MATADORS

Steve Bauman

ACKNOWLEDGMENTS

Any resemblance to actual people or places or products is coincidental, and the use of real company and product names is for literary effect only and definitely without permission.

Special thanks to Tatiana Gill for her editing and proofing help. She fixed a bunch of my typos. The remaining ones are all me.

Apologies in advance to Vermont. It's really an awesome, awesome place.

CHAPTER ONE

Subject: Reconnecting
From: Mike Norton
To: XXXXXX XXXX

It's me. How are you? Good, I hope.

Oh boy, where to start? It seems like you'd normally go with something casual and slightly mundane, carefully crafted to make it seem like you don't have an agenda before oh-so-cleverly easing into the real reason for sending an out-of-the-blue catching up message. But really, what's the point of fucking around? I know this is a mistake. Last time I did this, I said it wouldn't happen yet again, but here I am, like clockwork. Another looming anniversary, another embarrassing attempt to re-connect with the past.

A past I can barely remember. You know me and my terrible memory, right? I mean, I can't even remember if I can remember the things I've supposedly forgotten. Har. In all seriousness, there are enormous gaps in my life, decade-long ones. What I remember most of all was the feeling that life was going on elsewhere without me. For example, I can barely remember anything before I was ten, save for some hazy images of my sister flying a kite in awful green pants, of attending a World Series game with my father in 1977, of my mother being drunk again and me hiding in the closet and crying. There's the long, useless hours spent in the back yard throwing baseballs against a hard, cold brick wall, the dream of playing with anything resembling competence diminishing with each pitch in the dirt or in the neighbor's backyard, of sitting in my bedroom alone playing Atari VCS videogames while listening to Vin Scully cover the Dodgers. Most of my twenties were spent working fourteen hour days to further my career at the expense of any form of social life, though there may have been an all-expense-paid river rafting promotional trip somewhere in there, and pining over girls never talked to. Lots of pining. I could be a full-frame house with all of that pining. That's an exaggeration; it's more like a nice end table's worth.

With few, if any, known witnesses to any acts of heroism or cowardice during those years of beige-colored nothingness to recount those tales ad nauseum and permanently embed them into my brain, I'm left wondering if those memories are my own or if they're borrowed or stolen from fictional or non-fictional lives.

What's the point of all of this talk of memory? I don't know. I've been writing and rewriting this email for hours. Not that I can even be sure you'll ever read this, as I highly doubt you're monitoring this account. It wasn't your primary e-mail back when I set it up for you, and I haven't checked its status since you left. For all I know, it's full of all of the other messages I shouldn't have sent over the last ten years—their status either read or unread—and spam. Lots and lots of spam. Are you in the market for discount refills of your V1c0d|n, or maybe a faux Rolex to replace the 99-cent "I Love Lucy" watch you bought and ironically wore to our wedding? That sentence probably guarantees this will end up forever filtered.

Anyway, I hope you're doing well. It's been a long time. My brain is firing off in a million different directions, and instead of sleeping I'm sitting at my computer, desperately trying to reconnect. Isn't it ironic that we have a wealth of tools available that are designed to connect and re-connect us with others—our blogs, tweets, texts, cell phones, laptops, instant messengers, iPhones, etc—but we're more isolated from each other than ever? We spend hours typing on laptops in coffee shops and texting while waiting in line at the grocery store or methadone clinic under the guise of connecting with our virtual friends and lovers while ignoring everyone within ear- and eyeshot. We walk down streets with our ears stuffed full of iPod ear buds, blocking out the sounds of the street and providing us the perfect soundtrack of our own creation, and we're surrounded with people doing the same; God forbid we might be accidentally exposed to someone or something that expands our already insular views. Instead, we've turned that over to algorithms from Pandora or amazon.com, where people who are just like me like A, B, and C, and therefore I will be inclined to like A, B, and C, as well as D, E, and F, never mind that X, Y, and Z would also be super interesting to me if only I'd just unplug for one minute and open up my goddamn eyes and ears.

Maybe I'm just a crank, and old-timer railing against

new technology. Get off my lawn...! In my day...! It just seems like these tools have done nothing to bring us closer together; if anything, they've made all of us even more socially retarded, unable to translate all of that virtual connectivity into something more tangible and real. To compensate, we try to break out of our prisons of loneliness in the worst and most awkward and embarrassing ways imaginable, attacking things from weird angles and looking for solutions in the wrong places from the wrong people at the wrong time in order to connect with anyone.

Keep in mind that I'm not talking about the connections you have with family members; of course you're supposed to connect with them. It's part of the deal, right? They give birth to you, they raise you, they protect you, they occasionally give you nice things, they occasionally tell you that you don't suck. Obviously this isn't quite the case for everyone, for various sordid reasons that aren't really worth repeating or discussing. I mean, my own family members are like these people I know and love but sort of avoid, through no fault of theirs. They're decent enough people but I've never been able to connect with them on any meaningful level beyond what's obligated, what's required, the biological imperative that's probably built into our DNA. Despite this, I still feel some connection to them, however shamefully slight.

I'm also not talking about the ones you have with day-to-day people, which are fleeting and interesting but hardly transcendent. For example, I have friends and acquaintances, and we share some interests and/or enjoy doing things together, but I'm not sure I have a real connection with any of them. What's missing is something deeper and more meaningful. Maybe you can only connect with people as friends when you're a teenager, when the stakes are considerably lower and you're way less fucked up and self-conscious.

When I think of connections I inevitably think about the bond you and I had when we were an us. It's the kind you make with your closest friends and lovers, those people who finish your sentences and bring calm to the chaos, who speak in some secret language that only the two of you can understand, or the difference between merely great and transcendent sex with the people you're fucking. We connected the moment we entered each other's lives, and you remain the only person in my life that I've ever had a connection with on that level, and I remain connected to you even though we're no longer together. Honestly, I don't want these messages to be the only way I connect with you. I still want you back in my life, to talk to you, to sit next to you, to comfort you, to fuck you. I know that won't happen, obviously, but I can't help it; it's what I want, and I know it's not healthy. I know it's hurting me, it's keeping me from connecting with anyone else. Your ghost haunts me every day.

Is it like this for everyone? Do normal people have lives that are defined by the things which haunt them, the losses, regrets, things they chose not to do, things that were taken from them, the mountains of decisions made or not made, the vast chasms of guilt they wish they could fill, the forests of regret they'll never have a chance to clear? I think we're all like this, even if we won't admit it. We have ghosts haunting all of our waking and non-waking hours. Some are enormous and obvious; others insignificant and inconsequential. We do our best to be normal and ignore them, and days and weeks and years pass with them sitting on the sidelines never causing any trouble. We wake up, go to work, eat our dinners, watch some bad TV, go to bed, and our lives go on. Some choose to linger in the shadows and appear only when we're at our most vulnerable, like lonely summer nights, rainy days in fall, those periods during the dead of winter when the temperature never gets above freezing, or on holidays when everyone is expected to be full of happiness and cheer and the haunted feel like it's okay to not be okay.

Some people are better than others at keeping their ghosts at bay. Unfortunately, my ghosts are like Slimer from Ghostbusters. They aren't content to just hover around the edges; they're serious troublemakers. They're out of control, creating chaos around me every day, keeping me up at night, and making me feel confused and angry. When they're at the peak of their nefarious activities, when they're parading through the elegant banquet hall that is my life—you know, only with less elegance and more clutter—I have no idea what I'm going to be doing or saying next.

(Incidentally, I'm aware that using an extended Ghostbusters reference like this qualifies a perfectly reasonable example of my current state of confusion.)

In all seriousness, "they" told me that my ghosts would go away, that I would stop feeling their presence every single day. To some extent, "they" were correct, whoever "they" were. (Multiple actors of varying skill levels have taken on the challenging role of "they" over the years. It's currently in open casting, though no one's showed up for the audition.) Over the last 10 years, there have been times when Venkman and Stantz and Stengler had all of my ghosts in their containment fields and storage facilities, and I started feeling relatively normal. I was able to eat my dinners, keep my kitchen tidy, watch a reasonable amount of TV, and sleep the sleep of the content. I was good. Over things. But then something inevitably happens, some event or memory triggers the day-to-day equivalent of the dickless Walter Peck flipping a switch and releasing all of my ghosts, and I'm unable to contain the fallout. At that point it becomes impossible for me to send them away, I'm unable to stifle any emotions, and I just fall apart. Years ago, when I had more people around me for support, I didn't want people to think I was totally unstable, so I'd suppress everything. They were trying so hard to be there and offer comfort that I didn't have it in me to make them feel ineffectual by telling them how horrible I really felt.

Like most cowards, I've been spending the last decade running and hiding from my ghosts, but they've returned to the forefront. Every single year I'm reminded that I'll be living this day, this anniversary, over and over again for the rest of my life, and it doesn't bring me much peace. It reminds me how not good I really am, and the parts of me that I felt were out merely of balance when I last contacted you, that were precariously bobbing back and forth even then, have finally tumbled over and crashed. Words like "anxiety" and "depression"—as defined by Wikipedia, not by an accredited therapist—seem accurate, in that I'm less interested in things I used to be interested in and can't so much as get my mail without careful deliberation.

As they say, shit just got real, yo.

In the past, I'd be on the first train out of town, mentally checking out with alcohol or whatever I could get my hands on to assist myself in staying as unconscious as possible until it was tomorrow or a week from now, but something has happened that's made me want to fight. I feel like it's time to climb the steps of the Temple of Gozer the Gozerian, in an ill-fitting jumpsuit with Proton Pack in hand, and directly confront all of my ghosts.

(I promise this is the last Ghostbusters reference— have you even seen that movie before? Seriously, it's still the shit.)

I'm normally not this manic, but I feel like I need to get some things off my chest. It feels like something has ended and something has begun, and I'm kind of hoping that by working through this right now, I can figure out what exactly those somethings are. I realize this isn't the best time to do it or the best method, but it may be the only time and the only way to do it. I don't want you to be worried. I'm not asking for help. There are so many things I want to say and share, but there's no perfect entry point to everything, no logical flow and order. In lieu of that, I'm just going to dump out the contents of my brain here as quickly as possible. I'm going to say things I should've said years ago and things I probably shouldn't say today or ever. I'm going to be 100% unfiltered, which is probably unwise and potentially unwholesome. It's important for me to do this, for you to know everything. And maybe, just maybe, this process will give me the ammo to send all of those pesky ghosts away for good.

Apologies in advance for any typos. I know how much they bug you.

—

Now listening to: "Ghostbusters" - Ray Parker, Jr.

Subject: Where to Start?
From: Mike Norton
To: XXXXXX XXXX

So anyway, I was violently jolted out of a deep, alcohol-enhanced sleep at eight this morning by a ringing phone. My own. I receive so few calls that I barely recognized the sound. I answered it as groggily as possible, to reinforce to the caller that I was rudely awakened, that I'm not happy, and that it would be a very bad idea to ever do this again. I was hung over, and it was one of those bad ones where you worry that there may be a dead body in the living room.

"Mike, it's Blake," a chipper voice said.

Blake is someone you will learn more about as this story progresses, but for now just realize that he's the very last person on the face of the earth I wanted to speak with. I'm fairly certain that I groaned something positively Cthulu-esque, like "aarrghhhbaaaarrrgggle

Ph'nglui mglw'nafh wgah'nagl fhtagn," which would've received the subtitled translation of, "Hey. What?"

"I just got back from a run. Your waterfront is gorgeous at dawn."

This is one of those things I will thankfully never know.

"What happened to you last night, man?" he asked.

"I wasn't feeling well...."

"Liar," he said with a laugh. "I saw you chatting up that sweet little thing outside. You get lucky?"

I glanced over at my empty bed to make sure I didn't actually get lucky, at least the "she spent the night in my bed" kind of lucky.

"That was some night," he said.

I decided against asking him if he slept alone in his hotel room or if one or more of the lucky women he was chatting up last night was still asleep in his hotel room or possibly fumbling around looking for their car this morning while still drunk. Or I should've asked if he'd called his wife or spoken with his kid this morning. That would've really fucked with him. "Oh yeah," is all I said.

"I wish you'd stuck around."

"Sorry, you looked like you were fine on your own."

"Yeah, I was fine," he said with a tone that suggested the possibility of sex with multiple partners, or that he had a very pleasant evening of conversation and went home content and satisfied. "Look, I have a meeting in the late afternoon, but it should be done by five. Let's get some chow tonight, something mellow."

I would rather eat tinfoil and pour acid over my tongue. "Sure," I think I hear myself say.

"How about we meet up at seven-ish?"

"Sounds great."

"Okay."

"Okay."

I hung up and went back to a deep, dreamless sleep. An hour or month passed, and I was awakened again by a thump. I tried to ignore it. I heard it again. Still ignoring it. The thumps rapidly increased in frequency. Goddamnit, I hate living in an apartment. I don't mind the lack of space, and really enjoy the lack of responsibility for fixing things when they break. But the noises, the inconsiderate neighbors who don't answer their doors when the landlord shows up to evict them or the inconsiderate rackets they make at inappropriate hours, as in when I'm trying to sleep. Those I mind.

Thump thump.

It was loud. Consistent. Rhythmic. It was coming from my front door. Shit.

I crawled out of bed, light-headed and achy, and slipped on a pair of frayed sweatpant shorts, the kind fat people wear because they're oh-so stretchy. I could hear heavy machinery in the parking lot. I opened the door.

"Can you move your car?" a man I'd never seen before asked. "Cars have to be out of the lot for paving. We gave you the notice two days ago."

Shit. He was right, I'd forgotten. I apologized profusely and excessively. I briefly wondered how I got my car here last night. I could still taste sweat, possibly someone else's, and alcohol, also possibly someone else's, on my breath.

"It's okay, it's okay," he said. "Please move the car."

I grabbed my keys and walked out to the parking lot. The Escort wheezed and spit and coughed up blood before starting on the third crank, the engine's arrhythmic burbling coming of the exhaust a sure sign of imminent catastrophic failure. A group of surly men stared me down; one turned to say something to another, and they all laughed. I assumed they were currently diagnosing my car's problems, and computing the chance it would explode before I had a chance to get it to the curb. I parked at one of the metered spots on the street. I didn't have any coins, so I'd just have to hope that the meter maids wouldn't be active on a Wednesday morning.

I stumbled into my apartment, groggy but wide-awake. I sat on the futon in the living room and stared at the TV, which was off. When you were living here, this room felt cozy and inviting. You added dashes of color in the form of those wall tapestries you loved so much, and with those unframed abstract Kandinsky prints. Now it's back to being as uninviting as before, like I'd just moved in and couldn't be bothered to unpack. There are boxes in the living room, boxes in the bedroom, boxes in the kitchen. The walls have been stripped bare of color, and none of your vibrant baubles are collecting dust on the shelves. Just a few books, CDs, DVDs, and videogames, though the neon green Xbox 360 game cases provide some contrast against the cheap black veneer surfaces.

I could hear machinery whirring to life outside, and loud and deep voices giving directions. I got up and opened the door to the closet, digging out a box filled with papers and notes and items, the physical remains of our relationship. I carefully removed the top layer and found another box; it too was filled with random pieces of you and me. It seemed like our entire time together could be found in boxes within boxes, and you could spend an eternity searching through them without ever finding what you were looking for.

I found the receipt from our first date, dinner at NECI

Commons, $33.94. I found the ticket stub from my trip to London, and the notebook I'd filled with embarrassing and overly earnest, albeit heartfelt, poetry about and for you. I found the handwritten directions you gave me on how to get to your mom's house in Lyndonville. I found a Middlebury notebook, with a cursive message on the cover, "I Love You." I found the mix tape you gave me, called "Cheez Whiz and Gush," and the one I gave you in exchange, Manic Pop Thrills Vol. 1.1. I found The Verve's "Urban Hymns," and remembered how the CD was inexplicably our soundtrack, and when our relationship ended, I ended my relationship with the CD, leaving it behind for Radiohead's "OK Computer;" it sulked, it dyed its hair black, and it disappeared for years behind a bookcase. I found the flyer from the Huntington House Inn, where we stayed one night in the week after graduation. I found two photos of us standing on the waterfront in Burlington. I found the announcement note we prepared but never sent.

Everything that matters to me can be traced back to one evening in August of 1999 and the year that followed, but it's been long enough that I can't always tell whether or not these vivid and concrete memories of you are real. Did our conversations take place exactly as I remember them? Is everything in the right sequence? I can remember big moments and I think I can remember small ones, but more and more of the specific details are slipping away with each passing year unless I constantly conjure them up and go through these very exercises of remembrance. Did you own a red sweater? Did we go to Shelbourne Farms and get stuck in the rain? Did you have a tiny tattoo on your right ankle? No matter how many times I pour over the tangible things of yours, the pieces of you that remain in my possession, I can't say with any certainty whether I'm recalling actual memories or merely echoes, memories of memories intermixing with movies or books or TV shows or other bits of pop culture that I've somehow absorbed and turned personal.

I quickly shoved everything back in the box. I was always afraid of telling about the violent jolt you gave my life when we met. I knew nothing about you, but within seconds of meeting you, everything changed. You made me feel like anything was possible in the world. I've never been able to decide whether I should thank you or hate you for taking my hand in yours that night and saving me.

I briefly considered taking the box outside and throwing it into the dumpster, permanently deleting you from my life like some random file on my computer. Drag, drop, right-click, Empty, good-bye. Instead, I've left you in the Recycle Bin, restoring you when needed.

—

Now listening to: "The Sun Goes West" - The Faraway Places

Subject: State of Me
From: Mike Norton
To: XXXXXX XXXX

I don't think you'd like me if you met me today. I'm ashamed at the person I've become. I'm maxed out on my credit cards, and each month it's harder and harder to pay my rent. I'm not childish, but I don't act like an adult. I still have no concept of mortgages, 401Ks, sons, daughters, parent-teacher meetings, or dinner parties. I've fallen into extremes of routine. It used to drive you nuts, but it's gotten worse. The comfort I used to feel in routine has turned into a necessity, that if my routine is disrupted in any way I'm out of sorts for days or weeks.

My alarm goes off every morning at 7:37 to the rocking sounds of 99.9 "The Buzz," Burlington's alternative music powerhouse that's an alternative to anything that doesn't feature guitars channeling early 1990s grunge. The unusual time is intentional; it's off just enough from 7:30

to keep me from thinking I'm getting up too early, and an odd number because even times don't feel right. I get out of bed and head directly for the shower. I shave (Mach 3, Kiss My Face Mint Shaving Lotion), apply deodorant (Edge Sport Scent, three swipes), put on my clothes (drab and inexpensive), and walk to work at 8:14. I stop at Common Grounds for a large drip that promises me a trip to some exotic South American locale but usually leaves the same bitter taste in my mouth as any cup of coffee. I spend the next 8-10 hours pretending to enjoy a job where I help people find books and DVDs and gifts for mothers or fathers or nieces or nephews and tell them that no, that book isn't eligible for a three-for-two sale and that no, they can't use that coupon for that particular item. I haven't taken a vacation since the time we went on our New England tour, and I never take sick days. I'm an otherwise unremarkable but extremely reliable employee who's always available to work extra hours or take someone else's shift when they have a hot date or family event to attend. In other words, I'm an ideal candidate for advancement into the glorious world of management. I have yet to receive that particular promotion, however.

After work, I walk home. I take different paths, which keeps the walk from getting too monotonous. On Mondays, I stop at Green Mountain Co-op and buy a rotisserie chicken for dinner. Tuesday night is for leftovers. Wednesday, I try the co-op's buffet, where you can frequently find flavorless vegan cuisine sitting uneasily next to overcooked bacon that's practically exploding with greasy goodness all over its tofu-riffic neighbor. On Thursdays, I pick up a copy of Seven Days outside the store to see what matinee I might try to see over the weekend and heat up something from the freezer. On Fridays, I stop at Leo's for a slice. Upon arriving at home, I get my mail. I turn on the TV. I check my TiVo. I watch anything good that's been recorded while eating dinner. I do the dishes. I check my e-mail. I spend most evenings online indulging my compulsions: playing games, surfing websites, or doing both simultaneously. Between midnight and 1:30AM, I go to bed and try to sleep. Most nights, I'm unable to turn off my brain and stare at the ceiling for hours while fighting off my ghosts. Other nights I sleep the sleep of the content.

My days off pose a unique challenge. Because I'm a senior associate, I have most weekends off. The difference between a weekend or mid-week day off is largely lost on me; one has mostly married women and college students at the grocery store or laundromat, the other has a considerably larger number of people of all stripes and ages in the same places. Regardless, it's critical to treat all non-work activities like actual work. Each has to be scheduled, completed, and tracked, whether it's vacuuming, masturbation, grocery shopping, TV watching, crying, laundering, or panic attacks. Without imposing this kind of structure on yourself, it's too easy to take breaks and think, and with thinking comes the self-loathing that's the inevitable result of living a life where you feel the need to schedule and track these kinds of mundane activities.

The highlight of any day off is a trek to Church Street. I walk north on its red brick promenade, past various bars and restaurants, Banana Republic, and Ben and Jerry's, occasionally stopping at Crow Books to see if they have any interesting new used books. When I reach the

Unitarian church that gave the street its name, I loop back and walk past Borders, Old Navy, and then venture into the Town Center, where I alternate between starting on the top or bottom level, making a run through the mall and passing your standard mall staples like Hot Topic, American Eagle, The Gap, and all of the other places I can't shop at because I'm too old and too fat. I stop at the men's section of Macy's, looking for the optimal (and heavily discounted) item or items that will help externally define me to random passers-by who will choose to ignore me.

The spice things up a bit, I occasionally drive to Williston to shop at some big box stores, Best Buy, Bed Bath and Beyond, and their ilk. You wouldn't believe how that part of the state has changed since you were last here, all strip malls and chain restaurants and generic condos. I've never been able to figure why people want suburbia in Vermont. It's like they took my old stomping groups, the San Fernando Valley, and said yes, this is the model for how we want to live. People aspire to track housing and Wal-Mart? Why not embrace the old and funky over the new and plastic?

This routine, well... I'd be lying if I tried to convince you or anyone else that this is a particularly rich or rewarding way to live your life. If I was a better person— or to be more accurate, more like you—I would be helping the poor or homeless in my free time, especially since I'm one layoff away from joining them. Maybe I'd be volunteering with troubled teens or victims of domestic violence like you did, or at least teaching computers to the functionally illiterate. (As an aside, what does that even mean, to "teach computers?" You hear people talk like that: "I'm learning computers." Like what, how to turn them on? How to open a file? How to copy something? Babies are practically born with this knowledge today. Face it; if you're in that class, you're already fucked.)

Instead, with as few exceptions as possible, I always choose the safe and predictable, and strive to make every day like every other day. Except for yesterday, when everything went predictably south because of Facebook.

—

Now listening to: "Mr. Grey" - The Len Price 3

CHAPTER TWO

Subject: The Evil that is Facebook
From: Mike Norton
To: XXXXXX XXXX

You of all people know my aversion to socializing, how much I like to live hermetically sealed inside my own little weird world, only reaching outside of it on my own terms. It drove you crazy when we were together, it's only gotten worse in the last few years.

Yet I joined Facebook and created a profile under my real name, with personal information that can be viewed by almost anyone. For a while, I felt like I was in control of the situation. I added an application that tracks the movies, music, and books I like, figuring that might allow me to connect with cool people. But it only served to remind me how much out of touch I am with the tastes of my so-called peers. Which I'm fine with, so long as I can reconcile my desire to stop judging others for their awful,

awful tastes in everything with being able to easily see, every single day, their awful, awful tastes in everything.

I uploaded some random photos that apparently represent the visual history of my life on this planet, but it was obvious how I was coming up short. Everyone else has photos of them with others getting drunk on microbrews showcasing contrived attempts at spontaneous laughter and clowning around. They have pictures of themselves taken by others in exotic locations they've visited, or they're with their friends in Cabo in shorts and T-shirts and sunglasses, with big smiles, white teeth, tanned skin. Others have photos taken at weddings full of new possibilities and no regard for the horrific divorces that will inevitably follow, and baby photos that even I'm not cynical enough to think anything worse about than believing babies are usually ugly. In contrast, I've been to a few places and taken the occasional photo of some random landmark, but there are no big moments or occasions, no photos with friends and lovers. I have a few self-taken snapshots that only serve as reminders that I'm getting older and fatter and even less photogenic.

(I'd posted a few photos of you I'd scanned on my computer, but took them down after I overheard someone at work say that I had a monument to an ex-girlfriend on my Facebook page. Fucking hell.)

I started posting occasional status updates, but they only reminded people of my existence, which in turn only served to increase the frequency of updates from others on my own page. How many times can I be bitten by a zombie or ignore a request to join a gang before dead? How often will some fucking puppy throw a bone at me? I started to worry about etiquette. Will someone hate me in real life if I ignore their friend request, or worse, will they even notice or care? How many right- or left-wing status updates can you post before it's acceptable for someone on the opposite political spectrum to un-friend you? Why is there only an "I Like" button and not an "I Hate" one?

I started to lose faith in the basic mental health of those around me. Facebook status messages aren't the place to look for a second opinion on the strange lump we found on our collective necks. They're not where we vent our dirty laundry about co-workers, spouses, children, or anyone else for that matter; chances are, they're on your friends list. And all of the updates with context-free affirmations like "[Person X] feels that every day in every way I am getting better and better"—which is as factually inaccurate as it is dumb—or "[Person Y]'s heart is always open and radiates love" don't make you sound positive or upbeat or intriguing or mysterious or deep; they make you sound pathetic.

The moment we adults create an account, we start acting like prepubescent teens again. We over-share, we get catty, we create drama. And those of us on the outside looking in at the over-sharing and the cattiness and the drama, oh we feed on it. It's the best seat in town for the spectacle of people having at each other virtually, and we're more than willing to clap or give a standing ovation at the moments when the lives of others collapse around and in front of us. When it's on the Internet, we have the advantage of rationalizing that it's not "real life," that the drama doesn't matter and we all just need to chill out.

On some level, that's accurate. We're all just faking it. We're posting pictures that make us look cooler or thinner than we really are. We're inputting our dates-of-birth so we can receive cheap validation on our birthdays from people whose validation we previously didn't care enough about to tell them about it in the first place. I turn 40 in three days and no one even calls me to wish me a happy birthday in the real world, which is sort of expected since I never call anyone on their birthday or post a "happy birthday" on their Facebook wall or click on "Like" on their shameless birthday announcement. There's a point where they stop trying to figure out your birthday because you keep dodging the question but all you ever really want for them to do is care enough to ask.

We're listing our relationship statuses so we can savor that magical moment when it changes for the positive—everyone gives you a "like" on the day you change from "single" to "in a relationship" or "engaged" or "married"—and it gives a simple entry point for people to check up on us and start the public healing when the opposite happens. I'm terrified that I'll find out that my girlfriend or spouse is leaving me through a status change.

We're sharing the mundane minute-by-minute details of our lives via our Tweets and Woofs and Blurbs and Blasts and Splats or whatever the fuck venture capitalists are funding and tech websites are hyping today, but what are we actually revealing? If we're smart, nothing. We should live in constant, mortal fear of revealing too much. There's no reason to keep secrets anymore because we're voluntarily divulging every moment of our lives.

In one convenient location, I'm cataloguing, organizing, and tagging my real life for anyone to see. Nothing will be forgotten or lost. It's all preserved, the highs and lows, the weird and the mundane. Though we may externalize our lives via these sites, they're our idealized ones. We can more easily pull this off online because there's no non-verbal cues to throw people off, no body language or tones of voice to show that we're all delusional liars. (God help us all when these things are 100% video; instead of everyone becoming a headline writer, we'll all end up actors.) We've created virtual avatars for our real lives, turning Facebook into a cruel massively multiplayer game of embarrassment and judgment. This makes it kind of like the real world except that we can now come up short against our peers in more easily measured ways. Instead of simply comparing and judging each other in the most superficial of ways possible—attractiveness, income, race, coolness, sports ability, political orientation, neighborhood—we now compare the number of friends we have, our levels in Packrat, how our slaves are doing in Plantationville, how much money we have in Parking Wars, and our scores on quizzes. It's like high school mixed with Halo, a cutthroat game of pure competition where the losers end up with a bullet in their head, only an overly-caffeinated thirteen-year old in Dubuque isn't the shooter; it's a self-inflicted wound.

It's gotten to the point that it's possible to imagine a scenario where Facebook or Twitter goes down for some indefinite amount of time and there are a rash of suicides across the country, with people claiming they're disconnected from the world. Their ability to maintain internal lives have atrophied to the point where they feel isolated and alone when left in their rooms without the daily updates of the people around them.

After a week, I realized that I barely knew most of the 37 people on my friends list. I didn't care about the mundane details of their lives any more than I believe they care what I'm thinking at any given moment, what books and DVDs I own, or that I've added 100 points to my Gamerscore. I barely care about these things myself.

—

Now listening to: "Picture Book" - The Kinks

Subject: Booked for Life
From: Mike Norton
To: XXXXXX XXXX

Did I tell you that I work at Borders? It's a paycheck, nothing less, nothing more. Anyway, I have to tell you this Facebook- and Borders- related story.

This one girl that works there, Shoshanna Ronson, is one of those art students who appears on the verge of passing out at any moment because she doesn't eat anything. She posted an oh-so humorous status update about the creepy old guy she works with, forgetting that she added me as one of the seven-hundred-and-thirty-three people on her friends list and that I'm the only person at our store over thirty. As with most our inopportune reveals, it scrolled off the page like every other meaningless data point, forgotten by all but those affected by its message, i.e. me. If you think about it, this is the only way to manage our new virtual lives; put out mass quantities of data to throw people off the scent of what's really going on in our minds. True, we rarely share everything with anyone, whether virtually or in the real world. We're all trained from birth not to trust anyone else, particularly not that creepy childless guy who lives alone on the corner. We're all aware how alienated we are from everyone in the real world, but we pretend we're connected with people in the virtual world. We think we're making these connections with others, but we have no idea what to do with them.

Until that update, I thought Shoshanna was at least indifferent to my existence if not on somewhat friendly terms. She's an odd duck, with heavily freckled arms and anime-red hair makes her look like a troll doll. She's almost impossibly skinny, the envy of every other anorexic girl she comes in contact with, and speaks in this weird low monotone that she probably thinks makes her sound deep but in reality just drives everyone batshit insane. Like every other Borders employee, she appears to care about nothing. She's also our best employee; she has upward momentum, as the common vernacular goes. Despite her apparently finding me creepy, I kind of like her.

I'm not all that fond of anyone else there. Everyone's infected with their own unique brand of crazy. It starts at the top with our wonderful managers and kind of seeps down. The District Manager for the area is in his 50s and insufferably pretentious. He doesn't even hide his disgust at those below him; I guess the hierarchy of retail middle management is all he's got. You want to slap him and say, "YOU'RE A DM FOR BORDERS, NOT THE GODDAMN CEO OF AN EVEN MODERATELY SUCCESSFUL COMPANY." Fortunately, he rarely drops in.

The General Manager is impossible and insufferable, always dressing in black and rocking the eighties-style ponytail while still in his twenties. He truly believes in what he's doing though, which makes everyone hates him even more than they hate me. We think he's bipolar, so we have Friendly Tuesday, where he'll be gracious; on Manic Wednesday, he'll go psychotic and berate you in the middle of the sales floor. Sedated Friday is when you ask for day's off.

This one 24-year old kid named Justin was borderline retarded, though his pot-haze demeanor could produce some laughs. He was fired for using hate speech against the customer, which was true in that he genuinely hated the customers. If they asked about "The DaVinci Code" or "Twilight" or "Atlas Shrugged," he'd ask them for the author so he could look them up. If they asked for Dr. Seuss books, he'd send them to the medical reference section.

Justin's personal tipping point, the one we all expect to occur one day, was when a middle-aged customer flicked a Lindor Ball wrapper at him after a seemingly normal and uneventful register transaction. "I ate this a while ago," he said. "Can I pay for it now?"

Justin, seizing the moment, successfully channeled all of his pot-depressed adrenaline into a beautiful, if not downright poetic, rant. "THIS IS NOT A FUCKING RESTAURANT," he screamed. "PAY FOR THE GODDAMN MERCHANDISE BEFORE YOU INGEST IT, YOU FAT FUCK."

This became the store motto for a few months, but needless to say, we had to fire the poor kid. "I'm sorry, dude," he told me when I gave him the news. Apparently, he'd been seeing Shoshanna and she'd been "acting king of PMS-y" that day, which fueled his anger. When I gave him the news, he shrugged his shoulders and said, "This sucks," and walked out.

The customers don't really bother me anymore. Most of them spend their time in the cafe lobby watching porn on their laptops or reading magazines while waiting for their parents to pick them up. On rare occasions, there are still little inspirational moments that make it seem like a more meaningful job, like when a child asks for help finding something for school or for some book that's like some other book they enjoyed. You think for a moment, ask the child their age, talk to them a bit about their interests, and connect them with something truly magical. A cynic could easily dismiss these moments as aberrations, considering their infrequency, but not me. It feels like you're passing something between generations, and it's a reason—maybe the only reason—to actually like selling books to people.

It's difficult to convey this to the mostly young and interchangeable and insane kids who spend six months here before heading off to better things. They no longer have any interest in printed media; if it's not online and skimmable and sharable, it may as well not exist. Instead of engaging with customers, they engage with each other only in their own little insular bubble world. They spend too much time sharing uncomfortable details about their personal lives with each other both at the store and online. I don't really care that Ashton allegedly blew Justin in the closet, which triggered his spat with Shoshanna, or that Kyle has banged multiple customers in the parking lot on his breaks. When they're not talking about their personal lives, they discuss important topics like whether there will be enough Lindor Balls for everyone at the next store meeting or if the new Rewards cards will clash with the old ones.

—

Now listening to: "Bright Future In Sales" - Fountains of Wayne

Subject: Memory
From: Mike Norton
To: XXXXXX XXXX

As the marketing says, Facebook is also way to reconnect with schoolmates you haven't thought about in years, though do people wonder why they want to connect with people they couldn't be bothered to think about or keep in touch with for those years? It's not like you couldn't have sent them a letter or picked up a phone and called them. Most of them still live in the same neighborhoods you grew up in, for Christ's sake.

This ability to connect with your past is how I ended up at the Burlington International Airport waiting for jetBlue flight 74 to arrive from New York's JFK Airport. Its precious cargo was one Blake "Bain" Bivins, a fellow Matador from Cal State Northridge, my former roommate, someone I hadn't seen nor heard from in over 15 years until he sent me a "Friend" request. It came while

I was trying to figure out how to delete my profile and, against my better judgment, I accepted. Within minutes, I got my first message from him. We immediately traded some e-mails. He even invited me to join his "Entourage." I don't even get HBO and I can't avoid that fucking show. We sent a few e-mails back and forth, carrying on in the typically funny-sad way of people in their very late thirties about the things that used to make us young.

After a couple of weeks the messages slowed, and I was happy to finally get on with my life and stop traipsing merrily down memory lane with old college friends. Unfortunately, a throwaway "we should get together" line, issued from the safety of 3000 miles of unlikelihood away, somehow became specific.

"Okay, let's do this," he wrote. "Let's make it happen."

"I don't have any money," I wrote back.

"I don't want money, you idiot. Let's get together."

"Why, are you dying?"

"Yeah, I'm dying. Cancer."

He isn't dying.

It turns out that he's the head of marketing for a company which is trying to more proactively connect with "youth culture," and was coming to Burlington to visit an ad agency who he thought would "use design strategically to build brand distinction through product, packaging, merchandising, and marketing communication" for his company's product.

I shit you not. He actually wrote something like this.

"I'm going to be in town in a couple of days," he wrote. "Let's get some drinks and catch up."

I wasn't sure I wanted to spend an evening with my past. I tried to figure out a number of perfectly credible excuses for saying no. I went through dozens of variations of being out of town, but I felt like I'd have to lie about it on Facebook too. Which of course would make my co-workers wonder what I was doing at work while being out of town.

I decided I'd meet him for drinks. It wasn't like I had anything better to do.

I spent the morning of my day off sitting in the corner of the Suds N' Duds, a new laundromat/bar combo that seems like a match made in singles heaven. My eyes drifted across its dull interior, the beat-up futon, the pinball machine, the Formica bar, and the small tube TV showing reruns of "Keeping Up With the Kardashians." It's hard to say if this collection of tackiness was intentional or ironic; who can tell these days?

I stared at a book I had little interest in reading, Pablo Neruda's "Twenty Love Poems and a Song of Despair;" sure, it's fantastic—I remember you reading its poems to me in Spanish one night—but it was a prop, a public display of pretension designed to attract more cerebral members of the opposite sex then provide any form of entertainment or enlightenment. In my Cinemax-addled mind, this is how the scene would play out:

"So, you like Neruda," she'd walk up to me and say.

"Oh yeah," I'd say. "I really appreciate his beautiful imagery."

"Me too," she'd say as she sat down and returned my stare. "Want to go back to my place and fuck my brains out?"

Ever since college, the grand plan was always to act pseudo-intellectual in public places as a way of meeting other equally pseudo-intellectual people. It was implemented in laundromats, in cafes, in diners, and in parks. Each arena had its own book choices: coffee bars, for example, were for really pretentious writers, while malls were for really popular but still critically acclaimed writers. As I get older, it seems like a decent approach for someone who isn't good-looking enough to show up and have women swoon, is too old to be youthfully cool, and is too young to impress women with status and money, never mind that I don't have enough money or status to impress women with money, and too much money to impress anyone with a lack of money. Despite trying this approach with different books from a variety of authors across the literary spectrum, it had never actually worked.

Today's plan of intellectual conquest was subverted by the weather. Even though it's still summer, it feels like fall is forcing itself in and making itself comfortable. A cold front moved in overnight, and a strong and steady rain had kept away the usual flock of college-age women who populate places like this during the week. The only other person doing laundry right now was a twenty-something wearing a ridiculous outfit, a shiny silver shirt with large Japanese characters and pants with straps hanging from them that say, "Caffeine." They're so baggy at the cuff that he'd probably do a flying nun imitation after a strong updraft. When he walks by, he sounds like Velcro.

I was doing my best not to look my thirty-nine years, trying to seem like a viable alternative for some intelligent and insightful twenty-something. I was bedecked in my finest faded and slightly torn jeans, a lived-in j.crew sweater with a frayed collar that was too expensive to replace, and beat-up Doc Martens. My head was freshly shorn of hair, my facial hair neatly trimmed but not overly fussed with. This is slacker high couture, the chosen look for people who try extremely hard to not look like they're trying extremely hard. I tried extremely hard to cultivate the look.

As I got more tokens, a woman entered, softly cursing as she bumped her elbow on the front door. Dripping wet and clothed head-to-toe in black, she was exactly the kind of woman I find myself immediately drawn to: mid-to-late 20s, tall with short dark hair, light complexion, trendy dark glasses, a womanly figure with a few extra pounds properly distributed in all the right places, an off-the-floor look to her dress. She wasn't traditionally pretty, but you could tell that once you got to know her she'd be beautiful.

I returned to my seat and watched her over the top of my book. She unloaded her clothing, starting with her underwear—cotton, in multiple colors—and other garments, black bras, khaki shorts, T-shirts, cargo pants. I watched in anticipation of the moment she would break-free from the tyranny of domestic work and, upon noticing my smoldering intellectual coolness, walk over and begin an intellectually stimulating conversation that would inevitably end with the two of us falling madly in love with each other.

She briefly made eye contact with me after she finished tossing the last of her clothing into a second washing machine. Realizing that it's pretty creepy to watch people unload their clothes, I immediately looked down at my book, which had been perpetually stuck on the same blank page for the past ten minutes. She turned and walked out of the building, leaving Caffeine and me to our sulking. I perked back up when she returned a couple of minutes later with another basket.

She walked up to me, and my heart started beating. She smiled at me as she stepped up to token machine, inserting a five-dollar bill into the machine for 24 tokens.

"Great weather we're having," I cleverly said.

"What?" she looked up.

"Uh, this weather's nasty, isn't it?"

"Yeah, it's pretty bad."

She walked back to her basket. It was filled with men's clothing: a pair of torn Levi's, a flannel shirt, a couple of dress shirts, and fucking Fruit of the Loom tighty whities. When she finished, she walked over to the bar and bought a Peach Snapple. She sat down on one of the futons, tucked her long legs under her chin, pulled out her phone, and apparently started to text the Great American Novel to someone.

I decided I could never love a woman who would be with someone who wore lame underwear.

I looked at my watch. I still had two hours before my boring but controllable and predictable life was about to collide with my new and exciting and unpredictable and uncontrollable Facebook life in terrible, terrible ways.

—

Now listening to: "I'm Not A Kid Anymore" - Sloan

CHAPTER THREE

It was cool inside the airport. I struggled to button my coat—the one you liked so much back in the day—as it's a bit tighter around the midsection this year. I tried to mellow out, to look calm and cool, like this was just another day in an exciting and fulfilling life of gallivanting around town and the world, picking up friends and families at airports.

Bain entered the terminal carrying a small, stylish laptop case. He hadn't changed one bit. He was tanned, with stylishly long, thick blonde hair and a perfect complexion. A long, black overcoat covered his charcoal suit, and both looked vaguely designer-y and expensive. He wore a button-down dress shirt that was open at the collar, exposing a beaded necklace. A strikingly beautiful, square-jawed woman with cruelly short hair and broad shoulders trailed him, elegantly dragging expensive carry-on luggage.

Bain spotted me and waved. He turned his head slightly and said something out of the corner of his mouth to his companion. She laughed.

"Michael Norton," he said, throwing his strong hand around my wet fish of one. He grabbed me in a bear hug. "Well goddamn, it's good to see you."

"Um, yeah, good to see you, Bain," I said to his right shoulder. "Please let go of me."

"What kind of name is Bain?" the square-jawed woman asked.

"God, no one's called me that in years," Bain said.

"Really?" I said.

"You get too much sun there, big guy?" Bain asked me.

"God, no," I laughed. "Why would you even ask that?"

"Your head is totally sunburned."

"No it's not."

"It's beet red."

"Shut up.

"No, it really is," the square-jawed woman said.

"Oh, that." I was embarrassed, which may or may not have made my red head redder. "I'm taking this vitamin supplement... it causes that." I read on the Intarwebs that high doses of over-the-counter niacin (as nicotinic acid) can lower cholesterol levels, though no one seems to know why. It was good enough for me, since the alternative way of lowering that LDL involves losing weight and exercising, neither of which is easily integrated into my current lifestyle.

"You don't look so hot," Bain said.

"He's right," the square-jawed woman said. "It's not a

good look for you."

"Thanks."

Even after all of these years, he still towered over me, even though I stand about three inches taller.

"Are you going to introduce me to your red friend?" the square-jawed woman asked.

"Forgive my manners, dear," Bain said. "Alysia Flower, this is Michael Norton, the guy I was telling you about on the plane. Michael Norton, this is Alysia Flower. She's a lesbian."

"Blake, dear, must you introduce me like that?" she said with a hand gesture best described as a flourish.

"Hi," I said to her. She looked me over with an intense lack of interest before resuming her surveying of everything else within eyeshot that wasn't me.

"Um," I mumbled, "are these your only bags?"

"No," Bain said. "Let's go play some carry-on roulette. Let's see if I'm a winner!"

Bain and Alysia continued their conversation. I couldn't exactly parse out what they were talking about. They used words like "positioning" and "vertical integration," or something to that effect. They spoke the language of professionals, of people who have meetings in boardrooms and prepare Powerpoint presentations, people who regularly travel for work in stylish business suits and meet interesting people on planes while pounding down mixed drinks that their highly-paid assistants somehow slot into the "meals" section on an empty expense report. I am not currently, nor have I ever been, one of these people.

"How was your flight?" I said, hoping to get them to stop talking in that foreign tongue.

"It was great, smooth as can be out of L.A., which is

where I met Ms. Flower here." He smiled at her and she smiled back.

"Yeah, that flight is usually pretty mellow," I said. "It's better than United 177 down through Dulles, which is usually pretty turbulent, and US Airways through Philly is usually okay, but never fly Continental through Newark or LaGuardia, they both...."

They were both staring at me.

"I used to fly a lot... for work." This wasn't quite true. While searching for Bain's arrival time, I found a website that monitors and rates all in-bound and outbound flights for every airport. For some inexplicable reason, I found myself researching flights to and from Burlington. And for some even more inexplicable reason, I'd committed the results to memory.

"Darling, I have to pee," Alysia said as she headed off to the restroom.

"Don't leave the airport without saying good bye," Bain said as he watched her walk away. He turned to me, the first time he'd given me more than a cursory bit of attention since first arriving. "What do you think of Alysia?"

"She seems interesting."

"So check this out," he said very seriously, as he started to act out a scene. "I'm already in my seat and I spot her getting on the plane. We made immediate eye contact and I could tell there was a spark. Turns out she's in the seat next to me, and is also in marketing. We hit it off immediately and had this amazing conversation for the entire coast-to-coast flight and its connection. What are the odds?"

"How many seats were there on the plane?"

"So Mike Norton... Mike Norton...." Bain patted my

head like I was a puppy. "What happened to your hair, man?"

I sighed. "Fuck you very much for noticing."

He laughed.

"Wait, I have a joke for you. Do you eat pussy?"

"Well, I, wait, what?"

He slapped my stomach. "Must be the only thing you don't eat."

I caught my reflection in a window. I saw my bald head (too shiny), weak chin (too clichéd hipster facial hair), cherubic face (too puffy), and round stomach (too protruding). I looked tired, the skin under my eyes pouched. I became extremely self-conscious. Could Bain feel desperation oozing from every pore of my body? Could he tell I was the kind of person who had no one to share his life with, no prospects on the horizon, and nothing to eat in the fridge? Could he detect that I was the sad version of myself that I'd always feared I'd become? The type of guy who, three days ago, went to the doctor because he felt a lot of pressure in the area around his heart, who had an EKG and was poked and prodded a bit and had some X-Rays taken, and was told he was okay though his blood pressure was a little high and that he needed to lose some weight and was pre-diabetic. The same type of guy who, the next day, received a call that said that upon further review of the X-Rays, they discovered a mass in his lung area, that an emergency CT scan was ordered and scheduled and eventually skipped by him because he didn't want to know the results.

"Hah, funny," was all I could say to Bain.

"That's wicked," he said as he pointed to a Burton snowboard advertisement on the wall. It had some snowboarder doing some sort of move that seemed to defy the laws of physics. "These guys know their audience, and how to talk directly to them in a language they understand. I'm meeting with their agency tomorrow to see if they can take my next thing to a whole other level."

I couldn't believe this was coming out of the perfectly teethed mouth of the person who dragged me to see some band named Nirvana with when they opened for L7 at Rajis in 1990. At that moment, I hated him with the passion I usually reserved for people I don't know who look and talk like him.

"How often do you hit the slopes?"

"Are you kidding?"

"What are you doing in Vermont if you don't ski?"

"Hating snow."

"You should do it, man. Me and a bunch of friends went to Vail last year, rented a cabin for a week, shit man, the stories I could tell you...." He ran his hand through his hair. "I don't even remember half of it, know what I mean?"

"Nope."

—

Now listening to: "I Hate My Generation" - Cracker

Subject: Bain of My Existence
From: Mike Norton
To: XXXXXX XXXX

You're probably wondering who Bain is, and why I hadn't mentioned him before. You know how when a relationship ends, you're forced to divvy up your friends? Most of our mutual friends chose you over me, or more accurately they stopped interacting with me in any meaningful way after you left. This made perfect sense since they weren't my friends to begin with; you brought most of them with you. Maybe I had some idea of this arrangement in advance, so I never told you about Bain. This was a good thing—you probably would've insisted on taking him, despite never having met the guy. Chances are, he would've picked you too.

Let's back up to 1986. I'd initially balked at going to college, not really knowing why I'd go there and what I'd accomplish. Swept up by the Reagan 80s and inspired by Michael J. Fox's character on "Family Ties," I thought I'd try my hand at being a business major, despite not knowing what exactly a business major was. (To this day,

I still don't. I believe it has something to do with business.) I did, however, know that I wanted to be a young Republic business type without the Republican parts as it was the path to untold riches. Unfortunately, I had one strike out of the game: I went to a commuter school about 10 miles from my house, a monument to concrete called in the California state system in Northridge. It was all I could afford, or at least all my parents could afford since I wasn't a good enough student in High School to get any sort of scholarship, and my parents weren't poor enough for me to get financial aid. I knew nothing about student loans, but at under $400 a semester, tuition wasn't really a significant issue.

In the fourth year of my six-year stay, while under the influence of "On the Road," I decided that I too needed to hit the road and see the true America that existed outside the suburbs of Los Angeles. Unfortunately there weren't any trains in the area to hitch a ride on, and even if there had been, my idea of daring at the time was to occasionally cross over the hills that separated the Valley from scary Hollywood. Once I got over my romantic notions of hobo-ing, I decided to be a scenester. I went to every cool concert in town, from Jane's Addiction (before they were big) to Camper Van Beethoven (before they broke up) to Psych 101 who, when opening for Dead Milkmen, threw seat cushions at the audience at the John Anson Ford Theater. I was spit on at a Fishbone show at UCLA, and I blew out my eardrums for a week after Soul Asylum tore apart the Country Club in Reseda. I followed The Replacements for a week, mustering up the nerve to talk to Tommy Stinson once before a show to tell him that I dug his one solo song he'd play. ("Satellite.") I attended all of the concerts the L.A. Weekly told me I needed to attend, but I was a scenester in theory only; I never spoke to anyone, mostly standing by myself against the back walls of the venues while rhythmically nodding my head to the music. In fact, I was spending most of my days circling perilously close to the crowd of geeks with unfortunate tastes in clothing and impenetrable senses of humor who spent an inordinate amount of time discussing things that were on the opposite side of the girl-scoring spectrum. I had nothing against them; lord knows I was simpatico with their cause, and my tastes were aligned close enough with theirs to be a member in their club of social death. They should've been by de-facto support group, which would've at least put me in the company of someone, but my biggest fear was people thinking I was one of them. It took all of my power of faux-coolnes to not be them; I refused to read their comic books and fantasy or sci-fi novels, and I tried to limit my public Monty Python references to one a day. Instead of wearing their nondescript but tasteful clothing, I was the kind of guy who thought he could be defined by a concert T-shirt that was designed to imbue its wearer with the hope that some woman would see it and say, "You like the Pixies too?" and strike up a friendly conversation that ended with sex and love and marriage. If I couldn't quite suss out why I was attending college on a scholastic level, I did know that I hoped to find my dynamic future wife sitting next to me in some philosophy class, the bookish one that none of the macho frat boys would find beautiful but I would.

That never happened, but I did meet Bain, he of the dubious facial hair (which I shared), nerdy glasses (ditto), and self effacing manner we both used to deflect the obvious reality of our dorkiness. He was a lot like the faux-me but it came to him naturally. We randomly sat next to each other in the cafeteria, and silently acknowledged our mutual ditching and ate our forbidden but economically efficient nachos together. Such brazen flaunting of the rules! I called him Blake in those days, at least until some random girl at some random concert in 1991 gave him the nickname in because he looked a little like Kurt Cobain, what with his scraggly blond hair and fondness for flannel. We met in an Economics class in our sophomore year, though it would be more accurate to say we separately came to the same realization that Economics makes no sense and college professors don't care if you show up to class. Those who possess this knowledge are smart to turn tail, fly home, and buy nachos.

(Which, incidentally, we determined was the optimal meal for breakfast, lunch, and dinner because they'd opened a Taco Bell Express on campus that year and nachos represented the best quantity/value ratio. Ironically, we probably only concerned ourselves with such matters because of the Economics class we weren't attending.)

Over time, we continued to break away from the crowd and became our own two-man scene. Alone, we were invisible; together, we occupied more physical space. As we evolved our personas, we ended up like a certain type of college kid who dressed in thrift store clothes while taking English literature classes because we thought that's what we were supposed to do. We thought our world was doggedly bleak if not goddamn suicidal, and we'd tell anyone within earshot the moderately interesting stories that people always tell in social situations in the vague hope that they will make them seem dark and charismatic without necessarily being either. We were sensitive romantics, beautiful losers, bastards of young, but there was no real drama playing out inside our little suburban heads, though we wouldn't have minded if girls thought there was.

We got our ears pierced on a dare—the right one, which is to say the "left" one at the time, which wasn't the "I'm gay" one. The frat boys called us fags, but a few years later they'd all have their own ears and nipples pierced. We were frequently late to our classes, dragging our scraggly hair, torn 501s, band T-shirts of dubious cleanliness, and Doc Martens to school on our schedule, not one imposed by the man. Few girls found my brand of slackerdom even remotely sexually appealing, but Bain proved popular despite himself. In those days he was a good listener, the kind of person who could appear to find everyone more interesting and impressive than himself, and self-confident enough to think that girls he met might actually be interested in having sex with him.

He eventually realized that many of those girls were indeed willing to have sex with him, so he began to indulge them. He became effortlessly cool, his innate confidence never crossed over to cocky, and his inability to focus on anything turned laser-like when he found what he wanted, and what he mostly wanted was to sleep with as many girls as possible. Where I would spend an hour talking to a cute girl in the desperate hope she'd make the first move, Bain became the aggressor. Where I was waiting to react, he chose to act.

Unsurprisingly, he got laid a lot more in college than I did.

Bain and I spent most of the last two semesters hanging out at his place. We'd go out to see every live band we were told by Alternative Nation was cool and hip and edgy, and crawl back to his place at ridiculous hours in the morning. Sometime between concerts and waking up at 1PM, we finished college.

His apartment was a mess, filled with tapes and CDs, a prominent area devoted to his guitar, piles of L.A. Weekly papers that served as our bible—even though we'd deny it if anyone asked—piles of junk mail from every high-end store in the area, bills from American Express and Visa that he'd send off to his father, discarded photos from his time trying to impress girls with photography—considering the quantity of nudes, he'd been largely successful—and various beer cans. The walls were covered with stolen concert posters, stickers from Greenpeace and Amnesty International, and the same Che Guevara picture that remains standard issue for all budding college-age liberals. Unfortunately, neither of us smoked enough pot to justify the Bob Marley poster.

Bain's apartment was also conveniently located in Santa Monica, so it was closer to the clubs but a considerable hike from both my own place and school. It was a large bungalow that should've cost a fortune but was rent-controlled. After college, I formally moved in as we started our under-employed post-collegiate lifestyle. As a former rich kid slumming it at a state college in the Valley, Bain seemed to be scoring points by befriending an uncool kid from the valley. It set him apart from the other kids he grew up with, who were either insufferable preppies or insufferable hipsters. He hated both groups with an equal passion but didn't rule out fucking girls from both groups when the opportunities presented themselves. At the same time, I was using Bain as much as he was using me; I felt cooler by association, and it led to an occasional breadcrumb of toleration from girls who would otherwise never have given me the time of day.

We were going out a couple of nights a week to different concerts all over L.A., and Bain started sleeping with a lot of different women. I wasn't so lucky, only ending up with a single phone number from someone at a concert by The Wonder Stuff. An attractive girl walked up to me and handed me a napkin with a phone number after they'd closed their set with "Don't Bring Me Down, Gently." I called the number, but it turned out I wasn't the proper target; her friend had just given it to the wrong person. She meant it for my "good looking friend."

Bain ended up dating that girl for a while. Her name was Tasha. She was gorgeous, with thick lips and long blonde hair. With her came two more roommates. Her older brother Rich had a law degree but was "looking for work." He was an eccentric, to say the least. Bain and I went out a couple of times with Rich, but he drunk-danced like a retarded dervish; you could always find him by the large gap in the floor he created. He'd approach girls at a club and say things like, "how would you like to be bitches in my kennel?" "have you ever cleaned an AK-47?" or "have you ever skinned a ferret?" He actually expected to hook up with these girls, but who'd want to sleep in a room that consisted entirely of rows of cheap plastic Wal-Mart bookcases covered floor to ceiling with sci-fi and fantasy books, carburetors, and gun parts? Nevermind the pile of hay in the corner he used as a bed.

Irish Sean was a slightly different brand of crazy. He had narcolepsy and scoliosis, and one leg was longer than the other, so when he got drunk he walked in circles. He wasn't the brightest bulb in the box; for example, he once had a lengthy argument with Bain about how to turn off the power to the toilet. He spent most of his money at strip clubs and insisted that the best way to enjoy a lap dance was to wear sweats so they could really enjoy your erection. The only time I went to one with him, I had to endure his walk of shame when he went to a room for a lap dance, and then emerged moments later with the stripper as they walked over to the ATM to pay for said lap dance. The stripper was his favorite, a girl named Candy who had most of her teeth and, on this particular day, an enormous bruise that covered her entire thigh. "A guy was rough with me last night," she said. "I usually take ecstasy but took some MDMA and was fucked up, and he knew I was kinky, so I ended up with this."

When they weren't out getting drunk, they were in their rooms getting stoned. They spent all of their money on booze, pot, and strippers; it wasn't like they were paying rent. In fact, money was a real problem. I had started an hourly job at a computer company doing technical support, making more money than I'd ever made in my life but not enough to pay Los Angeles rent, but no one else had a regular paying gig. Bain occasionally showed up at a local record store, getting paid $6.50 an hour to listen to music and act surly whenever someone asked if they had something he deemed beneath his superior music tastes. Tasha waited tables at the Olive Garden, poorly. She was so bad at it, they'd cut her days down to two a week. Rich and Irish Sean were "between gigs, man" as they would say.

I ended up buying most of the groceries and paying all of the utilities on a place that I had no real connection to because the lease was in Bain's parent's name. And when it came time to collect the rent, I made up the difference when it inevitably came up short.

The concert going had slowed down, unless I paid for everyone's tickets. We saw Nirvana open for the Red Hot Chili Peppers at the Sports Arena, hung out and drank with Soul Asylum and opening act STP (who eventually had to change their name to Stone Temple Pilots) at the Country Club in Reseda before both broke big and become super uncool. We were seeing Soundgarden, Mudhoney, Screaming Trees, The Posies, and every other appropriate Seattle band that came through town. We weren't sure if we should still be seeing R.E.M. on the "Green" tour, we saw Elvis Costello a few times at the Wiltern, there was Urge Overkill at the Roxy and Paul Westerberg's first solo tour at the Whiskey, which remains to this day the best concert I've ever been to.

Everything on the surface was fine. Bain and I were still close, we still laughed, we still joked, we still bashed out the occasional terrible song in the garage, we consumed every bit of new music, saw all of the acclaimed movies, and read all of the right magazines and papers that told us which music and movies we should be consuming and seeing. But he was changing. He'd go for long drives in his Saab, returning a day later with bloodshot eyes and more parking tickets that he'd never pay. I'd constantly try to get some money from him, using the subtle tactic of saying things like, "Did you pay the rent yet? It's way past due." At this point he'd inevitably say that no, his big-shot lawyer father hadn't deposited any money into his account yet. He'd call his dad an asshole, say things like "what's a thousand bucks to a millionaire, can you believe that shit," and then change the topic to something considerably more important like, "There's gonna be this cool new industrial band at the Whiskey tonight. I hear they destroyed the stage at their last show. It'll be pretty intense." Then he'd ask me to take care of the rent and head off to wherever he headed off to.

One lazy Saturday afternoon, we found ourselves down at Venice trying to score tickets for some random poetry reading, but in reality we were just there looking for hook-ups (or in my case, just pine for everyone around me). Tasha was out of town, so Bain felt it was okay to have one-night stands, and that she fully understood and agreed with this setup. We sat on a wall near the beach and watched a group of Japanese students sitting at a table, talking in their native tongue, laughing at some joke that only they could understand. A large group of people had formed near the volleyball courts, and we watched them watching the matches.

A large group of tan college-age people walked toward us. They looked like the typical macho frat boy assholes that majored in beer drinking and date rape and ended up with Communications degrees. One of them glanced at Bain and did a double take. Bain stared at them, his head following their path.

"Blake Bivins, is that you?" one of the frat boys asked.

"Uh, yeah," Bain said. "Who are you?"

"It's Walt Christopher. We went to Rolling Hills High School together." Walt extended his hand. "It's good to see you."

Bain looked him up and down, from his white Reeboks to his cargo shorts to his impeccable hair. He stopped at the Greek letters on his chest and laughed. "Look at you," Bain said while hitting me on the shoulder like I had an idea what he was talking about. "Little Walt is all grown up and in a frat. How predictable."

Walt lowered his hand "Blake Bivins, still the poseur

STEVE BAUMAN

rebel."

Bain spit on the ground. "You were the fake one," Bain said, standing up like an exclamation point. "We used to smoke pot together. We used to ditch school together. And now look at you and your beautiful friends. Your type makes me sick, you sell outs."

"A sell out?" Walt said. "What does that even mean?" He puffed out his chest and walked right up into Bain's face, practically touching nose-to-nose. "Who are you trying to kid," he said softly and quietly. "Look at you, with your long hair that you probably spend hundreds of dollars on to maintain that slovenly look, and your messy clothes that are the height of fashion right now on the Westside. One of us is pretending to be someone else, and it isn't me."

Walt turned to his friends. "Let's get out of here. Nice seeing you, asshole." He began to walk away but was spun around by Bain's arm on his shoulder.

"What's your problem, Blake," Walt said as he turned around.

"You!" Bain yelled. "You're my fucking problem." A small crowd started to gather, a mix of sun worshippers and hipsters. "People like you walk around here like you own the fucking place, like you're God's gift to humanity. Look at you, you're all a bunch of worthless clones!"

Someone in the crowd said, "Yeah!"

Walt's face began to redden slightly and his hand formed a fist. "I suppose long hair and torn jeans and Doc Martens are original?" Walt said. "You maybe have a nice beat-up leather jacket back in the closet? Maybe some Chuck Taylor's, you know, the shit we wore in high school so we could appear fashionably poor. Now your friend here," Walk pointed at me. "By the look of his

6 0

clothes, I'm guessing he's closer to legitimately poor, but you Blake... you." Walt got back into Bain's face. "I tried living like that for a while, man. It's a waste of fucking time."

Two of Walt's friends ran up and pulled him away from Bain. Walt laughed. "I'm cool," he said as he shook off the grip of his friends. He began to walk away. "He always was an asshole," he said loud enough for us to hear.

Bain sat back down on the wall. Loud music could be heard coming from the volleyball pit, and people went back to smiling and having fun. Bain was sweating and his hands were shaking. "Let's go get those tickets," I said. "Everybody who's anybody is gonna be there."

Bain paused for a moment, collecting his thoughts. He ran his fingers through his long stringy hair. His hands were still shaking. "Let's go."

That always felt like a turning point for Bain. He became angrier, more hostile to everyone around him. His attitude toward women, Tasha specifically but to everyone generally, went from playful and fun to distrustful and misogynistic. He began viewing other guys as the enemy, and he'd dissect every guy that walked by in the cruelest ways possible. I was terrified to know what he was saying about me behind my back.

Bain and Tasha's relationship fell apart in a spectacular fashion. When they weren't arguing about money and breaking up, they were having loud reconcilement sex. Eventually, Bain started accusing her of having sex with every man she met. He tracked her movements, secretly following her as she went to the mall to shoplift underwear or to the store to buy beer. He opened her mail and looked through her purse. He asked her trick questions about her day-to-day activities and assessed the credibility of her answers. Even though I never really liked Tasha, I felt sorry for her.

She couldn't take it anymore, threw up her arms, and admitted to a non-existent affair. The fight was spectacular, and I'm pretty sure that Bain actually hit her, though I never had any proof. Regardless, Tasha moved out. Rich and Irish Sean stayed around, mostly because they weren't paying any rent.

Bain became even more insufferable. I'm not sure what dark shit he was doing on those nights and days when he disappeared; he always kept those details to himself. He'd pick up women in clubs, and rarely saw the same bedroom more than once. When he wasn't spending the night at someone else's house, I'd wake up and have awkward "hellos" with at least 3-4 girls a week. He'd spend most of his days working out, drinking, and shit talking the women who he slept with, ripping their entire lives to shreds for having the temerity to not be exactly like him. He reserved even more of his hatred for the ones who were like him, which has to tell you something about where his head was at.

This went on for most of the summer of 1993.

As Bain became more destructive, I had a harder and harder time spending any time with him. Since he was my entire social circle, I ended up spending most evenings in my bedroom watching TV, listening to music, and playing videogames while he went out nearly every night with Rich and Irish Sean. They weren't so much his wingmen as his comic relief; the more he riffed on their failings and pointed out how uncool they were—fortunately for everyone involved, Rich and Irish Sean were always too drunk and/or stoned to care—the more the women gravitated to him. They'd buy him drinks or drugs or clothes, or just outright give him money; he was the dark and troubled bad boy they knew they could save, a puppy by the side of the road. Only this puppy had a nasty bite, and when they failed or he got bored, he moved on to another victim.

This went on for the rest of 1993 and into 1994.

Work was going well enough, but I felt abandoned. It felt exactly like going from being a popular kid with lot of friends and social interaction in elementary school, to my unpopular days of junior high (or as you kids in Vermont call it, middle school). Seemingly overnight, all of it went away and I felt like a social pariah. Once I was no longer one of the cool kids, I turned inward.

When your twenty-five-year old self is longing for the days of when you were eleven, you know there's a problem. I was tired of the partying, the smell of smoke and booze lingering throughout the house and sticking to my clothes. I considered moving out, but to where? A shitty apartment in a shitty part of town?

There were occasional days when Bain would be the old Bain, and I'd have a glimmer of hope that things would go back to how they were, but they were fleeting. One day in 1994, I got a call from Marc Salzberg, the arts editor for Vermont Weekly. Apparently, he'd read my widely-tolerated column in the L.A. Weekly, one I'd been writing for the previous year, and asked if I'd be interested in a job covering the Vermont movie and music scene. I flew out for an interview and they offered me a job on the spot. I took a significant pay cut but it represented a new opportunity, a clean break from the past. I could live in Vermont and be whomever I wanted.

I left with barely a good bye. Bain forwarded my mail

for a couple of months, and I didn't hear from him again until we were united by the wonder that is Facebook.

—

Now listening to: "Serve the Servants" - Nirvana

CHAPTER FOUR

Subject: Baggage
From: Mike Norton
To: XXXXXX XXXX

Luggage began appearing on the carousel, everyone's baggage laid out in plain view for all to see. Why does everyone buy black bags? The desire to look cool and fashionable needs to be weighed against the impossibility of finding your own black bag amongst hundreds of identical ones. Give me a nice red plaid suitcase, or maybe a lime green Samsonite hard case that I can travel with ironically.

Bain rubbed his chin. I stared at his wedding band, a platinum number whose subtlety clearly masked its cost. "So, you got married?"

"You should know," he said. "I sent you an invitation."

He did. I'd forgotten. I don't do weddings, or at least I like to say I don't do weddings. The reality is that there haven't been any weddings to do or not do, other than Bain's. I've never been a best man, an usher, a page boy, a ring bearer, a greeter, a guest book or gift attendant, passed out rice, or collected weapons at the door. I've never escorted anyone down the aisle or given anyone away. I've never been to a bachelor party, given a reading or toast at a reception, or fucked a hormonal bridesmaid after they started playing "In Your Eyes" for the first dance.

"Right, yeah, sorry about that... I was traveling that weekend."

"Sure you were."

Bain removed the ring and slipped it into his pocket. He held his finger up to the light to show the faintest of outlines.

"The key is to take it off when you're tanning, or to make sure you put sunblock on your finger if you're going to be wearing it in the sun."

These are the kinds of things I'll never know.

"My wife totally runs my life," Bain said. "She's amazing, but it's great to be away for a few days. You know how it goes."

"Nope."

Bain gave me the quick overview of the last 15 years. After I left for Vermont, he got tired of his life of meaningless casual sex and partying and decided to get a full-time job. He said it just like that, like it was just a moment where he could flip a switch and go from loser to winner. He got a low-level job at an advertising agency, proofreading copy and running random errands. While he was doing this, he turned his attention to school and got an MBA and quickly moved up the ranks at the agency until he was managing multi-million dollar accounts.

He met his future wife, Jocelyn Sanchez, a "part-time model and actress, and full-time bitch" (as he described her). She was brown-haired, blue-eyed, and insufferably beautiful. They'd met at some party at some producer's house in Los Angeles, had sex in the bathroom, and somehow turned that into an 11-year marriage.

The square-jawed woman returned from the restroom. She barely acknowledged my existence.

"Mr. Bain," she said, stifling a giggle. "I must be going. Do call me while you're in our lovely little town."

Bain entered her number in his phone and promised her they'd meet up for drinks that week. They kissed each other on each cheek and said their good byes.

"You must show your friend Vienna, darling," she said as she walked away.

"Fantastic," Bain said as he watched her walk across the airport. He wasn't the only one.

"You're going to show me vacation photos?"

"No," Bain said as he pressed some buttons on his phone. "Want to see the most beautiful thing in the world?"

He held the phone to my face, and on the screen was literally the most beautiful baby I've ever seen, and I'm of the opinion they're all pretty ugly.

"You have a baby?"

"Yes, I have a baby," he said while flipping through some additional photos before putting the phone back in his pocket. "Her name's Vienna."

"After the city?"

"She was conceived there."

"Seriously?"

"No."

"So, Vienna?"

"Let me guess, you don't like kids."

"It's not that I don't like kids," I said. "It just seems selfish to want some smelly approximation of myself."

"Christ."

Bain's bags arrived. "You want to hang out here at the airport all night, or should we leave?" he asked.

I briefly considered what the nightlife at the airport might be like, with stewardesses and pilots and baggage handlers getting drunk and dancing and hooking up. It might be fun.

"Let's go."

—

Now listening to: "New Country" - The Walkmen

Subject: Day of Reckoning
From: Mike Norton
To: XXXXXX XXXX

In college, I was living an altogether more interesting life through, and occasionally with, Bain. Now, it's like he's from some alien world, one full of the rich and gorgeous and dinner parties and fancy suits and interesting conversations with lesbians.

"Nice ride," Bain said as I popped the hatch on my Escort.

I didn't want to know what kind of car he owned. Probably German. And fast.

I made room for his luggage, moving aside some boxes, jumper cables, and two containers of windshield washer fluid. Bain looked at my laundry basket. "I'm not keeping you from anything tonight, am I?"

I picked up his suitcase and angrily slammed it into the cleared area in the trunk.

"I guess not," he said.

The interior of my car was a mess, dominated by the subtle but permanent scent of gasoline. Bain had a "will this stain my suit?" look on his face.

"Get in," I said. "I haven't sacrificed any animals in here or anything."

"Funny."

The Escort started on the second crank, but my right wiper was fighting a losing battle with the late summer drizzle. The stereo came on way too loud, blasting "Tribulations" by LCD Soundsystem. I cranked down the volume.

"What is that?" Bain said.

"LCD Soundsystem."

"Never heard of them."

"Seriously?"

"Yes, seriously."

"I can't believe you haven't heard of them."

"Sorry."

"James Murphy is our age, and sings songs about people like you."

"Sounds like New Order."

"This song, sure."

"Eh, good music, but the dude can't sing."

I was a bit stunned. Bain was the biggest music fan I've ever known, a walking encyclopedia able to draw all of the parallels for every band from the Velvet Underground through Big Star, Game Theory, and the Chickasaw Mudd Puppies.

"Please tell me you dig Nickelback."

"Give me more credit than that," Bain said. "I saw Pearl Jam a few weeks ago."

I must've had an "I'm not impressed" look on my face.

"Oh, so my taste in music isn't cool enough for you any more?"

"No, it's not like that... I mean, you were always into some pretty cutting edge stuff."

"Yeah, and I grew up and stopped obsessing over the right music to listen to, or the right movies to see, or the right books to read."

"I didn't mean to imply anything."

"It's cool, man."

As Bain droned on about some other middlebrow concerts he'd attended in the last few years, I looked out of my window and saw that a spider had built an intricate web from the driver's side mirror to the side panel of my car.

We headed west on Williston Road across Interstate 89 into Burlington, past Hooters, Cheese Traders, and Higher Ground.

"This town is cute, in its own way" Bain said. "What do people like you do here?" he said.

"Not a lot, at least today."

"What's wrong with today?"

"It's Tuesday."

"So?"

"It's not exactly the most happening day of the week."

The spider had boldly left the mirror area while at a red light and was curled into a ball, apparently holding on for dear life under the buffeting of the winds. For a spider, this must've been the equivalent of standing in the middle of a tornado, only with fewer flying cows.

"This is a college town, right?"

"Yeah, the University of Vermont is on your right."

"Nice campus. It's no CSUN, right?" He laughed.

"The school of Paula Abdul."

"And the setting for many other fine movies, like 'Hiding Out.'"

"God, Ducky as a mob accountant, that was fine casting."

"Least. Convincing. Beard. Ever."

"I had a crush on Annebeth Gish," I said. "Still do."

You're probably too young to remember the cinematic masterpiece that is "Hiding Out." Jon Cryer plays Andrew Morenski, a successful stockbroker in an incredibly fake beard who has to testify against a mob boss. He's in protective custody because of death threats, and he escapes during a gun battle and ends up fleeing to his aunt's hometown. Once there, he cuts off his beard, dyes his hair in the most stereotypical new wave way, and goes back to his high school as Max Hauser because he's apparently into putting his family at risk and knows that the police and mob would never start their search with known living relatives. Once there, hilarity ensues. He enrolls in high school, re-lives being a teenager, tries to coach his geeky relative, falls in love with an underage girl, and ends up running for school president. After a climactic gunfight in the auditorium, where multiple students put their lives on the line for a liar, Ducky testifies and goes into witness protection. Conveniently, he ends up teaching at a college where the previously underage girl goes to school.

"They filmed the final college scene at CSUN," said Bain. "They made it look more, well...." He looked outside the car at UVM. "More like this."

"Anyway, my point is, we're near a college, so there have to be bars here... you know, places to mingle, full of young people to meet."

"Well, sure, but...."

He interrupted. "I'm thirsty. And I'm buying."

"Hooray for Tuesday."

—

Now listening to: "Hooray for Tuesday" - The Minders

Subject: Out of Control
From: Mike Norton
To: XXXXXX XXXX

I briefly considered taking a pass on the evening's activities and going on a search expedition for my arachnid hitchhiker, who'd bailed a half-mile or so ago. We'd have an adventure, searching for bugs or a new place to call home, but this boat had already sailed, and it was the Titanic and I was its captain or its Leonardo DiCaprio, and Bain was Billy Zane.

The rain had stopped. Bain was still talking about something related to leveraging or positioning or positioning leverages or leveraging new positional paradigms. Marketing is an alien language to me, thank God.

"This area looks fun," Bain said as we passed by the Church Street Marketplace.

"That's where we're going."

"Cool."

We came to stop at a brick-covered intersection, and we watched the pedestrians as they crossed. A stylish fat guy waddled across the street, like an egg in Prada. Assuming Prada comes in XXXL, and assuming a Prada suit looks like the black suit he's wearing. Regardless, it looks expensive and somehow he's the lone guy out there who's totally dry. He probably had his entire body permanently Rain-X-ed, or some other rich guy surgery, that keeps him from getting wet in the rain.

"Hello, look at that," Bain said.

A woman was crossing, trailing the Prada Egg and trying to get his attention. She was gorgeous and young. Her hips moved side-to-side, like she knew people were paying attention to her when she walked. Which they were.

"That's what success buys you," he said. "Do you think that woman would be interested in that man if he wasn't successful?"

"That's an amazing basis for a relationship."

"You gotta start somewhere," Bain said.

I flashed him a "you've got to be kidding?" look.

"Don't blame me, I don't make the rules. The first thing you notice about someone is how they look. Every social interaction starts with superficial judgments."

"So blind people are better than all of us sighted people?"

"Probably," Bain said as the intersection cleared and I inched the car forward. "Except for the whole 'blind' thing."

The entrance to the Burlington Radisson was empty. I parked behind a shuttle bus that was sitting under a flickering overhead light. Bain cursed at his Blackberry for not getting any reception as he got out of the car. When he finally got a signal, he sent a series of texts in rapid succession.

"What's this amazing product you're looking to have connect with Generation Whatever?" I asked.

"I can't tell you, but it'll be huge," he said without looking up. "Everyone will know what it is, and if I do my job right, they'll all want it."

I grabbed his bags out of the back of the Escort. "Please don't tell me it's another fucking iPod clone."

He laughed. "Not even close. It's not even on the same planet. It has something to do with music, but it'll make the iPod look like the Zune."

"So it is another fucking iPod clone."

"No, it's more than that. Way more." He looked up from his Blackberry. "Look at this," Bain says. He whipped out a new Powerbook and treated it like a fetish object, marveling at the lines of its titanium case. "Apple is delivering a consistent and unified message across all of its product lineup," he said. "No one can touch them right now. But me, I take these items, computers, phones, these pieces of metal and plastic, I turn them into something that lives in the hearts and minds of people like the ones in this room right now."

This would've been way more dramatic had the hotel lobby not been empty, save for the 50-year old woman behind the counter who probably wasn't the target demographic for his product.

"I help create an emotional connection with products."

I laughed. "Dude, it's just the shit we own."

He started the check-in process.

"This isn't a joke. Top brands are a lot more than that. They're like living organisms, adapting to their environments. They represent ideas. They have integrity. They express something. They create desire. They enter relationships, have values, and they have unique identities and personalities. They inspire a culture and change the world. They aren't just marketing constructs, though that's where my job comes to play. Everything I do is about connecting the brand with people through advertising, the web, viral videos on YouTube, Twitter, user blogs, and message boards. It's about applets on Facebook, or the sites that will replace Facebook. It's about getting celebrities to be seen with your items. It's serious shit, man."

It was an impressive speech, no question. Had anyone had been around to hear it, they surely would've stopped and listened, and possibly been inspired to sell out whatever idealism they still precariously held on to and take a few classes in shameless marketing.

"I'm going to throw my bags in my room and freshen up for a minute, call my wife, tell Vienna I love her, that sort of thing" Bain said.

"I need to park my car."

"Meet you down here in, say, fifteen minutes?"

"Okay, fifteen minutes."

Bain backed into the elevator. "You're lucky you don't have to deal with all of this wife stuff," he said.

Yes, that's what I say every day when I return to an empty apartment: I'm a very lucky man.

—

Now listening to: "Someone Take The Wheel" - The Replacements

CHAPTER FIVE

Subject: Black Mustang
From: Mike Norton
To: XXXXXX XXXX

One of my regrets for us is that we never found a bar, that neighborhood place where we could land regularly and hang out at the bar and have some cocktails and eat some mediocre food and socialize with other like-minded individuals and get drunk as fuck and blow it out, yo. It's the highly romanticized "Cheers" ideal, the place where everybody knows your name minus the name knowing and with shittier lighting, stickier floors, good tunes, and enough cool people to make us appear cooler by association.

"Where are we going to get our drink on in this fine town?" Bain asked, frowning at the dark and empty street next to the hotel. "Any good titty bars?"

"They're banned in Burlington."

"That's insane. How do you cope?"

I told him how they were an affront to women; undignified, tacky, exploitative, and one of the better paying short-term jobs for attractive women of various skill levels. (Admittedly, the last one doesn't really make a very strong anti-stripping point.) It reinforces certain gender stereotypes, is discriminatory, and it presents women's bodies as items to be bought and sold.

I probably didn't say all of that, though. In fact, it may have been, "I don't care. I don't get the appeal."

"Are you gay or something?"

"Look, if I want to go to a loud place full of hot women who despise me, I'll go to Abercrombie & Fitch and save money on the cover."

"Fine, no titty bars," Bain said, his voice tinged with mock-ironic regret. "So where are we going?"

"It's a place called Square Pegs," I said. "It's kind of a meat market."

"Like the show?"

"There's a show called Meat Market?"

"No, 'Square Pegs.' The show."

"No. Not like the show. Like square pegs don't fit in circle ones."

"Like Sarah Jessica Parker?"

I sighed, because I was already feeling dumber for continuing the conversation. "Yes, like Sarah Jessica Parker."

"Tragic hair."

"Tragic."

"Who played her friend?"

"Which one?"

"The hot one."

"Tracy Nelson?"

"Yeah, that's her. I'd still fuck her."

"Who wouldn't?"

"Now Sarah Jessica Parker," he said. "Great body, for sure. But horse faced, that one."

"Horse faced."

"Positively Seabiscuit-esque."

"So Square Pegs. Clever."

"Only the finest here in hippie town."

We headed west on College toward the Church Street Marketplace. As we crossed St. Paul, a black Mustang blew through the stop sign and locked its brakes at the intersection. The driver honked his horn at us as we crossed the street.

"Dick," I said under my breath.

Bain was having none of it. "What. The. Fuck," he said as he walked slowly in front of the car and stared down the driver.

"Get out of my fucking way," Black Mustang said as he poked his sweaty head out of his open window. His face was already red.

"I think I'll just stand here for a second," Bain said. "It's a beautiful night."

Black Mustang revved his engine. He'd replaced the Mustang's grill with barbed wire. It was very menacing in a very contrived and obvious way. Black Mustang probably wants you to believe his last name is "Danger."

"Let's go, man," I pleaded with Bain as I grabbed him and pulled him past the car.

"That dude's a dick," Bain said as the Mustang slowly idled past us.

Being called a dick was apparently the last straw. Black Mustang got out of the car, which looked like a Matchbox compared to his steroidal bulk. He left it parked in the intersection, with three annoyed but curious drivers waiting behind him.

"You wanna go, fuckhead?"

Bain stopped in his tracks. A small crowd of kids loitering in City Hall Park started to gather around. I craned my neck looking for Burlington's finest to come and save the day, but they were probably breaking up a fraternity party or smoking pot with the fraternity kids. As Black Mustang got closer, it seemed like he doubled in size. I'm not a small guy by any definition, nor is Bain. But Black Mustang was younger and bigger and stronger and uglier and meaner, and we were about to be stomped out by his Neanderthal boots. The first thing that popped into my head was whether or not I'd cleared out my Internet history. I'd hate to die knowing that the lasting image of my existence on this planet is my subscription to hotjapanesepanties.com.

(For the record, I do not subscribe to this site, nor do I know of its existence. I'm frightened of what I might find if I type it into Google. On a lark, I once Googled 'Burlington nude websites," wondering if a "Girls of Vermont"-style website even existed, and my shame search was exposed when it came up as an auto-complete entry when I let someone else use my computer. Needless to say, I have that shit locked down now. You can look at the computer, but never touch it.)

Instead of fleeing, Bain walked right up into Black Mustang's face. Black Mustang didn't flinch or back down, but neither did Bain.

"Let's briefly go over how this will play out," Bain said very clearly, very calmly, and very loudly. "You lay one finger on me, you get arrested for assault. I press charges. You go to jail." He started to play to the crowd. "Let's keep in mind it's because you almost hit me and my friend here."

Black Mustang turned redder, and clenched his fists. "I'm going to kick your...."

Bain put his hands up. "Wait, wait, wait, it gets better." He quickly pulled out his Blackberry and tapped a couple of buttons. "See this name on my phone here?" That's Robert Goldberg. You haven't heard of him, but he's a fucking shark of a lawyer. He'll be the one filing a civil suit against you, and based on your car and appearance, I'll probably lose a few hundred thousand when he wins. But you'll be bankrupted."

I felt flush. My heart started beating rapidly, and my chest tightened.

"So, here's your life from today forward," Bain said. "You almost hit two pedestrians who were crossing a street legally. You attack them. You go to jail. You're bankrupted by a civil suit. And why? Because you didn't say, 'I'm sorry.'"

"Fuck both of you," Black Mustang said as he got back in his car and peeled off down the road.

"Yes, yes, fuck both of us." The gathered crowd began clapping. Bain blew Black Mustang a kiss. "Good night, sweet prince."

Bain turned to me. "I'm starving. Let's get something to eat before we get our drink on."

—

Now listening to: "Street Fighting Man" - The Rolling Stones

Subject: Church of Retail
From: Mike Norton
To: XXXXXX XXXX

Walking down Church Street at night makes me feel old, more than it did when we walked it together back in the day. Even cold Tuesdays, which are otherwise quiet, are full of young couples and college kids looking hip and cool, and me wishing I was younger and hipper and cooler.

"This is a cute area," Bain said. "Kind of an unpretentious Third Street Promenade. You know, in Santa Monica."

"Yeah, been there. Lived near there. With you."

"Remember that time we were down there with Tasha and that girl you were trying to get with."

He's referring to Tasha's best friend Carrie. She was a beautiful girl, funny as hell, and with the most amazing taste in music. I was batshit crazy for her, and she absolutely completely tolerated me.

"One of those homeless dudes asked you for $5,000 so he could buy a truck," Bain said.

"I asked if he'd take a check."

Bain laughed. "Yeah, that was awesome."

"Carrie only hung out with us because she wanted to fuck you."

"Who?"

"Tasha's friend Carrie."

If there's been one constant in my life it's that I've always gravitated toward the impossible girls, the pretty and arty ones who were out of my weight class yet still expressed a flicker of interest over my own arty interests but turned and fled as soon as Bain entered the room, with his better looks, supposed better taste (I was the primary source of almost all of his interests and knowledge), and better personality. I'd wine them and dine them, and he'd swoop in and take the prize. I was their stopgap until something better appeared, their own "Plan B from North Hollywood." Bain would be a decent human being for a night or week or a month, get tired of their perceived clinginess as they tried to be that one woman who'd positively change him in some meaningful way, and then start the cycle of treating them like shit before kicking them to the curb. Then, to make matters even more annoying, he'd inform me that he was the good guy, that he'd actually done me a favor by detailing their tragic and extensive character flaws that made the merest thought of pursuing a relationship unpalatable.

I'd spent one glorious night with Carrie, not having sex of course; that wasn't ever going to happen with her, because she was perfection. As dazzling and much coveted as she was, it was obvious then that it was Blake she wanted. I was a consolation prize, an approximation. He had a one-week stand with Carrie after Tasha left, and the morning she appeared in my kitchen, half-naked and teary-eyed after he'd informed her of her uselessness to him, was one of the images I carried with me as I fled to Vermont.

"Carrie, right. We hooked up a couple of times. Great in bed, but kind of a bitch."

Carrie and I once went to a Replacements concert together at the Hollywood Palladium. This would've been 1989 or so. Both of us were into them, a lot, but Bain had abandoned them as sellouts for signing to a major label and for having the audacity to release "Don't Tell A Soul." Yeah, it sucked, but they were still the mighty 'Mats, my very own Beatles and Stones, a beer swilling band of fuck-ups with a gift for rock and melody and lyrics that spoke to my inner loser. I introduced them to Bain, of course, and he absorbed their back catalog and embraced their mythology like a true believer.

At the show, Carrie and I were in the mob that pushed closer to the stage as openers Royal Crescent Mob finished up their set of workmanlike white-guy indie funk. A half hour or so later, Paul Westerberg and company tore into the opener, "Talent Show"—a mediocre song on the record that sounded phenomenal live—and the sweaty crowd started to move in unison. What started as a gentle wave quickly got choppier, with rip tides and deadly currents. By the end of the song, I'd lost all interest in being close to the stage and pushed my way back to the far wall of the floor section. The only problem is that I'd lost Carrie. She'd had the same thought, and had fallen back earlier, and I never saw her again during the show. For the final encore, Paul, Tommy

Stinson, Slim Dunlap, and Chris Mars tore through the bitterest and most powerful version of "Bastards of Young" I've ever heard, and after that kind of majestic and life-changing performance, I was ready to claim Carrie. I eventually found her near the bar, making out with some Hollywood hipster douche. She waved me off as I walked up to her, so I went home.

"Where do you normally go?" Bain asked me.

"Tuesday is leftovers night."

"Leftovers night?"

"See, on Mondays I buy a chicken...."

"Stop, don't care. Where do we eat?"

"I don't know," I said. And I really didn't know. This is my least favorite question in the world. I've been known to cancel dinner plans at the merest hint of the question.

"Here we go," Bain said. "How about this place. Leo's Pizza? Let's get a couple of slices."

"I only go here on Fridays."

"Jesus Christ, dude."

Bain was aware of all of my youthful idiosyncrasies, but I could tell that he wasn't prepared for the new levels of weird that were oozing out of every one of my pores at an alarming rate. "This is fine," I finally said after a pregnant pause. "We can go here."

"Thank God, I was afraid I'd have to eat this lovely woman here," he said smiling at a college girl in tight pants and a tight jacket. She gave a shit-eating grin and looked him over head-to-toe before resuming her texting.

The fucker still had it.

—

Now listening to: "Bastards Of Young" - The Replacements

Subject: Crushed
From: Mike Norton
To: XXXXXX XXXX

Leo's has a distinctly different vibe during the week. It's packed on Fridays and Saturdays, letting me be buy my random slice with complete anonymity. Today, the dining area was empty and I felt sort of exposed and weirdly vulnerable, as if ordering pizza is the equivalent of getting caught masturbating by your mom or something. The only other people in the restaurant were a couple of kids eating slices at the counter and laughing. I could feel their cool, ironic, detached judgment deep in my deteriorating bones.

"Hi Mike, we don't usually see you here during the week," the server said to me.

She's not really just "the server." Her name is Janet. I've spoken to her a few times.

"Hi Janet."

"You look good tonight," she said, smiling. "Have you lost some weight?"

"Oh god no," I said, trying to figure out how to change the subject. I looked at my shoes, then the ceiling, then the walls, and finally back to Janet. "Busy night?"

"Nah, it's Tuesday."

Bain elbowed me. "Oh, this is Bain."

"Normal people call me Blake."

"Hi Blake."

"What'll it be for you guys tonight? Mike, you'll have two cheese slices, right?"

It freaks me out when people know what I order in advance. I don't like people exposing my routine. Take Uncommon Grounds: they started recognizing me and yelling out my order before I got to the register, so I stopped going for a month in the hope they'd forget me. When I went back, they still remembered so I was forced to switch from ordering a large Colombia Nariño Reserva del Patron to a medium Sumatra Mandheling, which I don't even like all that much.

"Make mine veggie," Bain said.

"Okay, two slices of cheese, two veggie. Anything to drink?"

"Just water for me," I said.

"Me too," Bain said. "We're saving up for later."

"I'll be back in a minute with your pizza," Janet said, and walked back to the kitchen to place the order.

"Well that was fun," Bain said.

"What was fun?"

"Seeing you flirt in your natural habitat."

"That was flirting?"

"It wasn't entirely unlike flirting," he said. "You're terrible at it."

"Thanks."

"What's with the lack of eye contact?"

"Sorry?"

"You looked at everything but her, the walls and floor mostly."

"I've seen her before."

"And you've seen the walls and floor before."

I started to mumble something, quickly realizing that things weren't going my way, but Bain interrupted. "But nothing. You have to look at a person to see them."

"What?"

"She was looking at you. She was seeing you."

I didn't want to play this particular game with Bain as I was already tired, and it was clear he was getting more and more frustrated over my inscrutability. Or maybe it was my searing intellect. "So what's her story?" he asked.

"Who, Janet?"

"You know her, right?"

Janet is thirty-seven, and has recently moved in with a friend because she's re-enrolled in school to finish her graduate work in psychology. She's kind and sensible and attractive, tall and slim and a little awkward. She's been through an early divorce and various unhappy relationships, which derailed her previous academic pursuit. She is openhearted, talkative, and always friendly, but it's all tinged with a slight bit of melancholy that suits me greatly. Like she knows she shouldn't be working at her current job but can't quite fight the inertia that's pushing her into her current rut.

"Yeah, I know her, a little," I said. "She's cool. I think she's married."

"She's totally interested in you," Bain said.

"No she isn't," I said. "She's never said anything like

that." How are you supposed to tell if someone who works for tips is legitimately interested in you? It's like dating a stripper or a webcam model. The power dynamic is all wrong. Are they being nice to you out of genuine interest or to extract more bills from your wallet?

"You don't wait for a girl to verbally tell you she likes you," Bain said. "It's the sparkle in her eyes, her posture, the way she grabs your head and shoves your face into her tits."

"What?"

"Ask her out, right now. Tonight."

"Oh God no," I said, laughing. "I can't."

"Come on, man," he said. "What do you have to lose?"

"It could be a disaster."

"It won't be a disaster."

"It could be."

"And an asteroid could hit the Earth tomorrow and we could all die," Bain said. "So what?"

"Exactly, you get it."

"I get what?"

"Asking her out is low risk, but the consequences of failure are high, just like your asteroid strike."

"Still not making sense."

"You know, the odds that one will hit the Earth are pretty low but the results would be really, really bad. Michael Bay bad."

"And this has what exactly to do with dating?"

"I'm a big supporter of mitigating the risks of failure so I won't have to worry about their consequences."

"How do you plan on mitigating the risk of an asteroid hitting the Earth?"

"You're the one who brought up the asteroid."

"I'm lost."

"If I ask her out and she says no, I'll be bummed. If I don't ask her out, I won't be bummed. See, consequences avoided through risk mitigation."

"So to you, asking someone out is like an asteroid hitting the Earth?"

"Again, your analogy, not mine." I paused. "But yeah, pretty much."

Janet returned to the table with our pizza and refilled our water glasses. Bain gave her a large smile, which she returned. She was already on his side. I stared down my food.

"Can I get you anything else," Janet asked.

"I think we're good here," Bain said.

"Okay," she said.

"Okay," Bain said, smiling.

I took another bite.

Janet walked back to the counter.

"Dude," Bain said. "Is it possible for you to be any less friendly?"

"Yes," I said. "Yes it is."

—

Now listening to: "Save It For A Rainy Day" - The Jayhawks

Subject: Social Life
From: Mike Norton
To: XXXXXX XXXX

Why do you think it's difficult to reconnect with some
people you've shared your life with, compared to others?
I've known Bain longer than I've known you, and Bain
and I lived with each over longer than you and I lived
together. He's this critical figure in my life; hell, he's
practically a mythological creature, my Zeus or Odysseus
or Thor or Batman. But it's extremely difficult to talk to
him, particularly compared to how we were back in the
day. I know in my heart you and I wouldn't have that
problem, that everything would be simple for the two of
us.

    "I feel like I've been doing most of the talking
tonight," Bain said as we continued to realize how little
we had to talk about anymore. "How are you really
doing?"

"Fair to middling," I said. "Maybe a C or C+, or an 80/100 on the videogame review scale."

"On the what?"

"Never mind, inside joke."

(You see, videogame magazines and websites regularly overrate mediocrity, so they end up with highly skewed overall ratings compared to music or movie publications. I know this because I read them. I'll stop now.)

"I'm sure that's funny," Bain said. "To you."

Ah, a bon mot of douchiosity! I'm humbled in Bain's presence, and react accordingly with something equally douchey that isn't worth repeating.

"So, other than not chatting up hot waitresses, what have you been up to all of these years?" Bain asked, trying to redirect the conversation from my continuous mocking of his level of douchitude.

"I'm trying to do a lot of nothing," I said, sitting back and smiling smugly, as if this is a valid lifestyle choice.

"That's a bold move for a forty-year old."

"I'm daring to be great."

"At nothing."

"It's what I'm best at."

"Seriously, what do you mean by 'nothing?'" he said, doing an amazing job at faking interest. It's something you need to be able to do at a moment's notice if you're to survive in the world of marketing or PR. "You're unemployed? You've never gotten laid?"

I think he expected me to talk about my social activities, but if I were being honest I'd have to say they're largely non-existent. I have no friends of my own age, and God help me if I start hanging out with twenty-something Borders co-workers. And when it comes to romance, dating is pretty much the hardest videogame in the world. As soon as I level up, there's another boss monster waiting to take me out, and I've spent most of my adult life searching for cheat codes that don't exist. I realize this all sounds a bit over-the-top, but I can assure you that I have some justification for thinking this way.

To use one recent example, I was set up on a blind date by a Borders coworker, who meant well but didn't quite understand the depth of my inability to be normal. I was told that the woman was interesting and nice and a little geeky, which sounded perfect. More women are embracing their own perceived inner geekdom, which means those of us who are actually geeks can be upfront about our terrible and embarrassing interests (typically finding out that how they perceive their geekiness rarely aligns with ours, so it's only moderately less awkward).

So anyway, I'm thinking that maybe, just maybe, I could've opened the date with, "Hi, I'm Michael, do you find any of the following geeky shit charming? Scary? Like videogames, comic book movies, The Simpsons, Futurama? Not that I am a geek, mind you, but I thought I'd ask as sort of an icebreaker."

I didn't do anything of the sorts, but we still had a decent enough time, with easy conversation and lots of laughs. She did align with me on some level; she was the kind of person you could text about cockpunching, and not only would she get it but she'd take it and run with it, creating cockpunching leagues, cockpunching cheerleaders, etc.

But she was much cooler than I expected, dressed in vintage clothes, intentionally tacky sunglasses, and she showcased the pale beauty and striking makeup of my eternally unattainable and inexplicable attraction, the Goth. This made me uncomfortable, of course, what with my collection of generic checkered shirts that even I can't tell apart.

After our date reached its end, I immediately told her I wanted to see her again, and she agreed to meet up for dinner two days later. That night, things were going just as well, and I started thinking she might even invite me back to her apartment. Instead, she ditched me after dinner the dreaded "emergency message from a friend who needs help, I'm sorry, I hope you understand." Maybe it was the Grey Goose on the first date that made her think I had some potential, because she never replied to another message or text.

Whenever one of these dating experiences doesn't prove completely debilitating, I feel slightly empowered and dust off my Internet personal ad in the hope of extending my social circle outside of my body's radius. I'll spend nearly ten minutes crafting the perfect me, attach a few photos that showcase my best features—being covered in flattering shadows—and as you might expect, I receive a flood of responses from attractive and interesting women of all stripes. The last time I exposed myself to the dating world, there must have been, wow, hundreds of people who skipped right past me to the guy who says he likes his dog and hikes in the woods every weekend when not skiing and/or promoting liberal causes. I hate that guy.

In reality, I got one response in the first month, from a nice enough woman named Amy inexplicably took pity on me and sent a "UR FUNNY"-style ice-breaking message. We exchanged a couple of random e-mails and decided to meet up for coffee. I felt no connection with her whatsoever, so I decided I would role-play. I would try to do and say whatever it took to secure a warm body to spend the night with. This would allow me to feel shallow and empty the day after as I contemplated why I bothered with something so shallow and empty in the first place. I suppose it was better than the shallow and empty feeling I'd normally be experiencing from staying home on yet another Friday night.

I knew I was being an asshole, which is why Project Asshole—my name for the project—started to unravel as soon as I arrived at the coffee shop. Sitting alone, waiting for her to arrive, I previewed the evening in my head in movie trailer form. Amy was 34, tall and slim, beautiful, with shortly cropped hair, high cheekbones, and a proclivity toward stylish sweaters that looked lived-in and comfortable. She worked in marketing, and enjoyed lots of outdoor activities like snowboarding, mountain biking, and hiking. She also liked working out, Sting, and world music. For the purpose of securing this date and advancing to the next level, i.e. at a minimum scoring boob, I too decided that I enjoyed all of those things. In fact, it was uncanny how much we had in common thanks to the Internet and Google and Wikipedia.

Since our actual face-to-face interaction was going to take place in the real world, without easy access to all of those powerful tools of faking compatibility, I was faced with one minor problem: We actually shared nothing in common. It wasn't just nothing nothing, but serious polar "not cute in that movie sort of attracting way" opposite. It's the record scratch moment of the trailer. I fully anticipated that we'd have only two things to talk about that evening, jack and shit. I was already going through our initial exchange and the subsequent Hindenburging of our burgeoning relationship.

I'd notice her walk in, looking at all of the tables full

of people she'd no doubt prefer to be meeting.

"Amy?" I'd ask as she walked up to my table.

"Michael?" she'd reply while doing mental gymnastics as she tried to figure out why I looked so much worse in person than I did in the altered photograph on my profile. My Photoshop artistry is legendary, and the MySpace angle works for guys too. Pro-tip: Assuming you don't have skin that resembles the surface of Mars, close cropping does wonders for hiding a double chin and/or jowls. "It's... nice to meet you," she'd say as we sat down.

"It's... nice to meet you too."

We'd make random small talk about parking, about the weather, about anything but this evening.

"So, what do you do again?" she'd eventually ask while planning an exit strategy that Pentagon generals would envy.

"I'm a writer."

"Oh, that's interesting," she'd say, surprised that someone like me was actually creative in any way. She'd perk up a bit, and you could almost sense a flicker of desire appear in her eyes. "What do you write about?"

"Mostly fiction."

"Have you been published?"

"Not yet."

The flicker would be extinguished.

If things were going really poorly, I'd be tempted to talk about my upcoming fantasy/sci-fi hybrid novel set in the world of Vas'jir. In "Book I: Apocryphae," we meet the main character Mikel N'ore-tun, a young orphan commoner who leads an insignificant life of little regard until his farm is attacked by invading hordes of Zelarian Mercenary Centaurs brandishing the Mark of Gazz'majeric, the accursed sorceress who was once banished to the Sepulcher of Il'Disrepairia. Mikel watches his neighbors be slaughtered by the centaurs and their invisible drakon, but is somehow spared when he confronts their leader with the words-which-should-never-be-spoken, causing them to flee in horror. Mikel hits the road with his talking dog Max and discovers an entire world in flames. By "Book II: Familiae Perpulit," he's joined on his journey by a wise old mage from the land of the Maedari named Ravian Halraen-Smythe, a one-armed pirate from Ghoglarath named Scarr Wiggin's, a feral witch named Bleumoon Rayne Stormcrow (who in "Book V: Feral Rayne," becomes his lover), and a charming sprite named Albie. Mikel and his band of brothers must make a dangerous journey across, below, and above the lands of Vas'jir in order to save the people from the reign of Gazz'majeric. In "Book III: Spun Heirlooms," Mikel discovers that he is the son of the once great King Praehiberem, whose rule ended with the great sundering that resulted in the imprisonment of Gazz'majeric. Over the span of the last four books in the series, Mikel discovers that he is the legendary Una, "The One," and that only he can send Gazz'majeric back to the underworld of S'cteliggog. Mikel becomes a vampire in "Book IV: Darkfall of Despair," and finds out that Bleumoon is descended from an alien race called the Danaglan in "Book VI: Heavenly Bodies." In "Book VII: Finis," he finds out that Gazz'majeric is his sister, and that his father is still alive. Bleumoon gives her life for Mikel but is reincarnated as a proper Vas'jir.

After telling her all of this, I'd remind her that I was still working on the ending.

"So," Amy would say while catching a secret look at her watch. "You make a living at that?"

"Not really."

"So, what pays the bills?"

"I work at Borders and do some editing on the side."

"Oh."

"Yeah."

"What kind of editing work do you do?"

"It's for a magazine."

"What kind of magazine?"

This is where I'd have to make the decision about whether to tell the truth or lie in the hope of getting cheap sex. If any hope remained, if the flicker had yet to be completely extinguished, I might talk about a travel magazine, something impressive and lucrative sounding. If I went with the fantasy/sci-fi tact, I may as well be editing "NAMBLA: The Magazine." The truth, unfortunately, isn't much better. "A computer magazine," I'd say, and the metaphorical cat would officially be out of the bag.

"Computers and stuff, huh?" she'd say, fidgeting in her chair. "Interesting...."

This would be followed by two minutes of awkward silence. Hopefully someone would get a drink, buy some sort of food product, or get shot in a drive-by.

"So, what do you do when you're not working?" she'd ask.

"Uh... well, I write."

"Well, yeah, obviously."

"And I like to read."

"Uh huh."

"And I mess around on the Internet."

"Right."

"And play games."

"Games?"

"Computer games."

"On the Internet?"

"Sometimes. Mostly I play games solo at home. You see, there are tons of games just for playing by your... self."

"I see."

Now there'd be another two minutes of awkward silence. Hopefully one or both of us will be consuming the food product or drink purchased earlier, or at least bleeding out from their gunshot wound.

"So, did you have anything in mind for tonight?" she'd ask.

"Sex, mainly," is what I'd be tempted to say. "I have no idea," is what I'd actually say. "I generally make a habit of avoiding this sort of thing for just this reason."

"What reason?"

Another two minutes of awkward silence.

"That reason."

"I see what you mean."

At this point, we'd both realize we'd made an awful mistake, wish each other luck in our future catastrophic blind dates, and head home resigned to never, ever, do this again. Which both of us would fail to do, though I can't speak to Amy's future successes or failures as I never heard from her again. I returned home, checked my answering machine, grabbed my e-mail, logged into the matchmaking service, and checked my instant messenger for any sign of her with no luck. However, Citibank wondered if I'd purchased something in Massachusetts two days earlier (I had), someone was telling me that my penis isn't long enough (it isn't) and that I could make thousands working at home selling diet bread (wait, what?), some 25-year old single mother named

SNUGGLES64 thought my profile was funny, and some girl sent me a link to check out her new webcam to see if she had what it takes to be a porn star. She really did have it.

—

Now listening to: "How to Fight Loneliness" - Wilco

Subject: Lies and More Lies
From: Mike Norton
To: XXXXXX XXXX

I didn't really want to tell Bain that I feel like my life is a never-ending sequence of Mondays, so I jumped off the cliffs of logic into the sea of stupid. I invented a me that I wish actually existed. I told him that I was working on my book, that I'd written multiple stories that were being published in various literary journals that were conveniently out-of-print and unavailable from any online e-tailer, that I have an agent in New York—he goes and asks who it is, so I make up some random Jewish woman's name (does this make me racist)—and that I have entertained a few phone calls with Hollywood types about turning something into a movie. It's the story of someone fabulously talented and interesting and aggressive and productive. I am none of these things, and none of this is true.

"Your Facebook profile says you work at Borders," Bain said.

Nailed.

"It's out of date," I lied. "That was just a part-time gig to pay the bills until I finish the book."

At that exact moment, Bain had me. He was coming in for the kill, ready to pierce my +5 Armor of Aloofness with his +3 Two-handed Sword of Penetrating Perception. God, I need to play fewer games.

"So are you one of those sad lonely men who never marry and eat frozen meals every night and are so afraid of rejection they won't even own a pet?" Bain asked.

"I have a fish tank."

"There you go. You have fish. That's something," he said, looking around the room. "Let me guess," Bain said, taking a bite of his pizza. "You go home every day, kick those Docs off under your scuffed coffee table, throw your shirt into a pile, slip into a tattered concert tee, grab a beer, slip your hands in your sweatpants, and call it a night."

"For the record, I don't own sweatpants," I lied. I told Bain that I actually liked being alone, doing my own thing. It was better for work, better for my lifestyle, such that it is.

"Only sociopaths want to be alone," Bane said.

I kind of went off at him this point, with some rambling speech about how what he said was exactly the kind of thing people like to say when they're trying to be profound. It's also patently absurd, on face value. Some of us are just wired differently. We don't need the constant validation of people around us. We derive our happiness from within. We explore our inner selves, we're introspective, we're contemplative, we read, we study, we learn, we listen to music, we watch movies and TV shows, we go places, we do things. We're not all bitter and spiteful. We just choose not to do these things with other people.

"Look, I go out, a lot," I said.

"With other people?"

"Yes, with other people. Women. Friends. Lots of people."

"Really?"

"Why are you so surprised?"

"I'm not, it's just odd that you haven't talked about anyone else this evening. No tales of drunken revelry with friends, vacations in exotic locations," Bain paused. "Adult things."

"I talked about Janet."

"That doesn't count," he said. "That was a freebie because we ran into her."

I was getting nervous. Bain had already pegged me for what I am today, a former dreamer who'd fallen out of bed. To compensate, I chose the path of cowards. I lied. In short, I continued the charade of the faux-me, the person I wish I was, that stupid college kid who tried to act cool but failed and withered in the presence of the great Blake "Bain" Bivins. What's more embarrassing, living the life I'm leading or feeling a compulsion to make up one just so be the kind of person who isn't living the life I'm leading? A better person would just say fuck it, this is me, love me, hate me, call me a loser. I don't care. Of all of the things in the world to care about, why is how others perceive me so important? It isn't like Bain is going to return to his life in California, call every one of our collective friends, and rat out my sad existence. For all I know, he's already done that; I have no contact with any of these people.

I told him stories about women I've slept with, quadrupling the number of faux-partners I've had and making them sound a lot less significant. Three isn't remotely interesting; a dozen is a good start, and a number over twenty is even better, at least the ones I could faux-remember from the last few years. I told him about faux-one-night stands that never happened, like the one with the dominatrix who drove a Pontiac Grand A. I laughed boisterously over the stories of faux-parties never attended, of faux-friends made up from scratch. I knew what buttons to press. I told him sexual details, gave him images of faux-tits and faux-pussies, and that seemed to satisfy his voyeuristic needs.

"So despite these adventures and relationships, these amazing stories" he emphasized the word "amazing" to the point where it was clear he wasn't buying much of what I was saying, though at this point I was beyond caring. "Despite them, you insist you're cool with being alone, and that it doesn't affect these relationships?"

I sort of dragged out a "right," not entirely sure where he was going.

"I say bullshit."

"Oh."

"You're a commitment phobe."

I cackled. "No, that's definitely not the problem." If he only knew, right?

"Then why are you still flying solo?"

"It's... complicated." I sighed. "It's not because I can't be with women, I love being with them, I love sleeping with them, I love their bodies, every type." I paused. "Trust me, I just love women, what can I say?"

"Who doesn't love women?" Bain said. His face

suddenly turned serious. "You want to try something really challenging? Try loving a woman."

I paused. "That's the dumbest thing you've ever said."

"I'm serious."

"Yeah, seriously dumb."

"Listen." Bain got even more animated. It started making me slightly uncomfortable. "Women aren't as complicated as you think they are."

"No, they're worse."

"They're not. It's really simple."

"Okay, Oprah, give me the 411."

He looked annoyed.

"Sorry, go ahead," I said.

"The trick is to stop thinking of them as women."

"That's kind of difficult, what with them parading their boobs around like they do."

"Cute. Look, you have common interests with them, you share things, maybe you become close. Assuming you have the right attitude and enough exposure to women in the things you do..." he trailed off as he looked me up and down, "which might be a bigger issue for some."

"Fuck you, fuck you very much."

Bain laughed. "Most guys think women are better than men."

"That's definitely true."

"You're wrong," he said, moving forward in his seat. "That's all on the surface. Women don't have any real power, so they have to be pretty and nice."

I laughed. "That's misogynistic."

"It's the truth."

"Assuming this is true, and that's a mighty big assumption, rich boy, you're saying that being nice is only part of an act?"

"You're missing the point here."

"So what is the point?"

"The point is, women and men are similar, and you need for them to believe you're their equal, but you're not. Men have all the power."

I stared at him blankly.

"You need to be confident, always state what you want, and become the center of attention all the time. Women don't want a wallflower."

"Not every woman is like that. Janet isn't like that."

"Trust me. She is. I know what I'm talking about. You follow those basic guidelines and rules and everything will be okay."

"Well thank you, Tony Robbins," I said.

"Who?"

"Tony Robbins? Motivational speaker? Ridiculous jaw? Impossibly tan? Taller than most NBA players? He probably gets laid even more than you..."

"He's a dick. I met him at this..."

"Oh fuck off, man."

"What?" He gave a look of mock indignation.

"You've changed," I said, shaking my head.

"And you haven't."

"I like me."

"No you don't."

I yawned.

"Am I boring you?"

"I was up writing all night," I lied. I haven't written anything in five years. "My book is coming along really well."

"I didn't know you were writing a book," Janet said as she walked up to the table.

I stumbled and mumbled.

"How's that working out for you?" Bain asked, maybe sensing my imminent collapse.

"How's what...?"

"You had a deal in place, right?"

"A book deal?" Janet said. "That's amazing."

I was boxed in. I wasn't sure what to do. I briefly considered owning up to my entire charade, but that seemed like it would require too much clichéd exposition about the supposed blazing talent who turns out to be not-so-talented and ends up amounting to nothing, disappointing all who believed in him along the way. You see this guy at high school reunions, the head of every club and social group, the valedictorian types who end up as used car salesmen. Not that there's anything wrong with selling cars; it's just there were an infinite number of possibilities in front of you and you end up with something so basic and mundane and disappointing to those who would choose to pass judgment on such things.

I was like this, only my talent wasn't so much blazing as it was a dimly lit ember on its way out. Quickly.

For the same reason I didn't want to tell Bain and Janet the truth, I never told you. It's embarrassing, it's depressing. To make a short story long, my widely tolerated column in college landed me a part-time gig at a "major print publication" in Los Angeles, which led to me winning a few awards, some talk about national syndication, and some minor notoriety that's been lost to history because the publication croaked without a viable Internet strategy and every piece I wrote went "poof." However, right before the "poof," I managed to secure a book deal with some minor publishing house that was looking to reach the young and sullen, and they fronted me like $20K when I was 24. It's amusing to think of the scale of this today, in the world of blogs and YouTube accounts where random people can reach millions of people by just screaming, "Leave Britney Alone!" It's totally fucked up the ability of people to be happy with modest viewers or readers, since it's so easy to be huge.

The money was my undoing. While Bain and I were on the outs, and our living arrangements were driving me insane, I had this new pressure of trying to manage a book on the side. I began to think life was supposed to be grim and grey and dour, and I was supposed to hate my life, my job, my living arrangements, and a lack of success and money was not only inevitable, it was downright noble. I was addicted to disappointment and underachievement, because it was easier to manage than success. I was lost about what to do with my life, even though I was given every opportunity to have some direction, but it was okay, it was all right. Everyone was confused and directionless at 24, right? So I flaked on the opportunity and left for a random editorial job in Vermont, which is what I was doing when we met.

Relative to the people I grew up with, I'm probably more successful than most. I was the one who got relatively good grades, who didn't spend all their free time taking drugs and fucking around, the one who went to college. There was Derek, who smoked all day and dreamed of one day opening a head shop. His girlfriend Sharon smoked with him and worked at Applebee's. Dave ended up living under a bridge near the little league field, his brains fried from drugs. Pucci ended up staying in the neighborhood, working odd jobs, and getting Sharon pregnant.

Compared to that lot, I'm not a complete failure. This is what keeps me running, even though another part of me wants to stop dead in my tracks and crash back down to earth. I can't get past the idea that there's something better for me than this, whatever this is at any given moment, because I can't not keep asking myself this question over-and-over again: What if I'm unable to find that something better?

"Can we get that bill," I said to Janet.

—

Now listening to: "Talent Show" - The Replacements

Subject: "Judge & Jury," Coming This Fall to TBS
From: Mike Norton
To: XXXXXX XXXX

I laid into Bain the second after Janet left the table to retrieve our bill. "I don't have a book deal, you asshole," I spit at him, sounding my pissiest.

"Sorry, man," Bain said. "I didn't know."

I told him that nothing had happened, that I just passed on the opportunity and we went our separate ways. It wasn't a big deal.

"It seems like kind of a big deal," he said.

I launched into a frankly ridiculous rant about materialism and using wealth as a sole barometer for success, blah blah blah. It was positively socialist in standing up for the proletariat, the poor starving artist, and the corruption of the bourgeoisie. You would've been proud. "Just because I don't have a fucking BMW..." I stood up, ready to bail on the evening. "Look, I'm ecstatic you have your shit together and your beautiful wife and perfect kid, and I know I don't measure up and all... but I don't need this shit right now."

"Dude, come on," Bain said, his voice calm. "Sit down."

I meekly sat back down like a kid who'd tried to leave the table before finishing his vegetables.

"I'm not judging you, man," Bain said, his voice oozing the faux sincerity of the marketer. "I'm just trying to catch up. That's it."

"Look, I've got my own thing going," I said confidently. "Just because I don't buy into the conventional definitions of success...."

Janet returned to the table, a broad smile lit up her face. "You guys doing anything fun tonight?" she asked Bain. Same old story.

"We're going to, where was that?" Bain said.

"Square Pegs," I told him.

"Square Pegs."

"Oh, that sounds like fun," she said, with a small laugh.

I could tell she was disgusted over the prospect of going to a place like Square Pegs. Definitely not her crowd, thank God. I wanted to tell her that I'd rather spend the next few hours shaving my back than hanging out with the college crowd, but Bain was commanding the conversation. "You should come by after work," he said. "Have a drink with us if we're still there."

I died, right there. You don't invite people like Janet—i.e. anyone with a brain that's over 25—to places like Square Pegs. Even I know that. I kicked Bain under the table. "He's kidding," I said.

"Oh," she said. "In that case, you boys have a fun night."

She left our table. I was embarrassed.

"You're an idiot," Bain said.

"I know."

"She would've come out with us."

"No, she wouldn't have gone to Square Pegs," I said. "It's not her crowd."

"How do you know what 'her crowd' is?"

"Look, I just know," I said. And I do know. She's smart, she's classy. She likes to go to Crow Books instead of Borders, because it has a better selection of books by people not named Dan Brown or Stephenie Meyer or James Patterson. Not that I have anything against those guys; I'm no book snob, though I've never read anything by any of them.

"Forget it," I told Bain. "We'll just have a good time."

"I bet she's the grateful type," Bain said. "She's perfect for you."

I should've walked out right there. It was one thing to insult me, but Janet deserved his respect. He'd leveled up in doucheness, from 3-series BMW owner to 7-series BMW owner. If he wasn't careful, he'd cross over to BMW SUV owner.

I looked up at Janet to see if she'd fully crossed over to the Bain party, returning to our table only to flirt and chat him up, but she was busy talking to the kids at the counter. She waved at us as we reached the entrance.

"It was nice to meet you, Janet," Bain said as we walked past the counter. "Good luck with school."

"Thank you," she beamed to Bain. "See you on Friday, right Mike?"

As much as I want to ask Janet out on a date—and I'm pretty sure she'd say yes because I'm pretty sure I made up her marriage and I'm pretty sure she leads me into asking her out all the time by saying things like "I have nothing to do after work" or "have you seen that movie yet? I'd really like to see it"—I've done nothing to deserve her. She's smart, she says interesting things. She's done interesting things, and tells interesting stories. I don't do anything anymore, and my stories are all ten-years old.

Or maybe I'm misreading things. Maybe she'd say no. I've lost the ability to absorb and read the moods and motivations of others through a kind of subconscious osmosis. Kids born without it are considered mentally handicapped, and people who have lots of it are called "charismatic" and become movie stars and politicians. It's not what they say; it's this energy they put off that makes us feel good about ourselves. I'm unable to do it anymore; I'm not convinced I've ever had it to any reasonable degree.

"Yeah, Friday." I lied. I kept my head down and slipped out of the restaurant. I'll never be able to step foot back into Leo's after tonight's debacle with Bain. I might even end up at Pizza Hut, even though I wouldn't wish that fate upon my worst enemy. I mean, what does Janet think of me now after that performance? Does she think I'm one of those aging players, desperately clinging to their youths by surrounding themselves with hipster youths? God knows she's probably wondering who Bain is, and probably wanting his number.

Before I got serious about thinking of getting serious about Janet, I spent months trying to decide whether or not to call another girl I meant online, Courtney, whose company I enjoy and whose bed I'd gladly share if she'd have me. We went out a couple of times, with great conversations that revealed highly compatible interests. I was afraid of coming on too strong so I kept waiting for her to call me; when she did call, I'd take the lead and ask her to see a movie, or to go out for drinks. We ended up going out dozens of times, but the only time I mustered up the courage to invite her to my apartment she said she had to feed her friend's fish. Let me repeat that one more time: "I have to feed my friend's fish." After that humiliation, I gave up all hope with her despite continuing our non-dating dating. The rationalizations can quickly: she's way, way too attractive for someone like me, which makes me feel like I'm boxing outside of my class. She's smarter and more successful than I'll ever be, she has more close friends than people I know, she has the kind of family I've never had, etc.

I talk myself out of almost every interpersonal relationship by going through similar checklists of reasons why I should stop before anything goes too far. I spend so much time obsessive over the inevitable humiliation that will inevitably occur that I'm barely able to have any sort of meaningful social interaction anymore. Years of rejection and self-criticism hasn't thickened my skin or given me the kinds of growth experiences that have resulted in learning to live with rejection (or rejecting someone else, for that matter), so I've chosen the path of least resistance, to shut out life altogether.

—

Now listening to: "Smog Moon" - Matthew Sweet

CHAPTER SIX

I have to admit that I envy the Facebookers and bloggers and diarists, who will have the luxury of never forgetting anything because of their obsessive documentation of their day-to-day minutia. Which is one of the reasons I wrote those messages to you in the past and why I'm writing all of these over the next few hours or days, or however long it takes to dump out the contents of my brain. There are some things I don't want to forget.

I've had a recurring dream about you for years. I first experienced it during what should've been our first Christmas together, when we were doing our best to remain broken up and miserable. In the dream, you're living on a commune somewhere in Western Massachusetts, walking barefoot across a grassy area in a long flowing skirt and an oversized T-shirt, your matted hair tied back in a ponytail. You have your eyebrow pierced again, and a new tattoo on your shoulder. You're holding hands with a thin and tan boy with no shirt and long, tattered shorts, and the tendrils of his dreadlocks reach the middle of his hairless back. The two of you are discussing serious topics, agreeing on every point, excited with your shared knowledge. You walk toward a stream, strip down naked, and jump in the water. You're young and beautiful and I still love you, but I'm unable to be there with you.

Though I like to pretend otherwise, things were never perfect with us. There were times when I began to question what the fuck I was doing, and by extension wondering what the fuck you were doing. Alarm bells were going off because of the differences in our personalities, even though I've never put too much faith in conventional rules of attraction. You're either compatible or you aren't, and we were merely at different places in our lives. You were still experimenting and exploring and I was more settled. A part of me wanted to share some of those experiences with you, but the allure of drugs and alcohol is largely lost on someone who doesn't like to feel out of control. I was in denial over the size of the gap that was opening up between us, and believed that once school ended, it would fill with, I don't know, nougat. Nougat made of compatibility.

I suppose I could've dwelled on those feelings, but I choose to focus on the fact that we both got past the, "what the fuck are we doing" moments, that we ended up together and in love despite, or perhaps even because of, those differences.

What else can I say about the time we were together?

That we were happy? That we filled slots in each other's lives that needed filling, and I don't mean that in a sexual way unless that works for you? That I felt incomplete before I met you and whole after? I'd always believed that true love could only come about after two people went through the motions of getting to know each other, exchanging their personal histories, their philosophies on life and love, their opinions on weighty matters such as boxers/briefs, the side of the bed they sleep on, preferences in toothpaste and which "Bewitched" Darren they preferred, and their brains would process all of that information while ignoring the input of the heart or other vital organs that are usually out to sabotage the whole affair. The fact of the matter is that I loved you more than I ever thought it was possible to love anyone, and that it was intense and one-of-a-kind and immediate. I mean, love at first sight is so corny, and not something I'd ever believed in until it actually happened. It's one of those myths perpetuated by the terminally unlovable, but the Internet throws a new wrinkle into things. It lets us be personal in an impersonal medium. We cover all of the important issues from the privacy and safety of our homes and, if desired, behind a veil of anonymity. It's like we all realize that we may never meet the person we're corresponding with, so we're free to share with these random people the most intimate secrets of our lives. It's like confession, without all of that Catholicism shit. We tell people the most embarrassing things we've ever done, go into details about things we've never told our closest friends, and casually discuss our sexual proclivities. (All conversations online, whether they occur in chat rooms or via email, inevitably turn into discussions about sex. Why this is the case is something of a mystery.) We do this while carefully considering every word, selecting each to deliver its maximum impact. In the process, we all become a sort of über version of ourselves, one cleverer, wittier, and more charming and interesting than we'll ever be in person. Since both people are doing this, it's easy for one or both people to become interested in the person's disembodied brain. When the bodies match what the brains have conjured, the combined effect is devastating, doing double-damage to the heart and other equally vulnerable organs. Which is what happened, I think, with us.

While it's true I have a terrible memory, I also have a handful of perfectly vivid memories that are stored somewhere safe in my forebrain for easy retrieval, my neural pathways and limbic system working in perfect concert. For example, I remember that you were "VTGrrl12"—so feminist!—I was inexplicably "doofus1234" (Clearly there were 1233 previous "doofus" profiles). When you said hi, and started telling me how interesting you thought I sounded, I wasn't entirely sure how to proceed. Then, as now, I was by most measures an average person. Not too smart, but also not dumb. I didn't excel at anything but could do a little bit of everything. I didn't consider myself a catch of any sort, having been single and dateless in nearly ten years. I was terrified.

We exchanged a handful of exploratory e-mails, you gave me your phone number and we took our virtual conversations to the phone world. After a few long calls, we decided to meet despite neither of us having so much as exchanged a single photo. That's unfathomable today, isn't it? Ten years ago, it made perfectly logical sense.

I go over the details of our first date in my head a lot, trying to keep its details so vivid that it may as well have occurred yesterday and avoid the memory atrophy that results in those multi-year gaps. We were to meet in front of Muddy Waters at seven o'clock on Friday, August 13th, 1999. Friday the 13th, were we mad? The previous evening, we both admitted a level of nervousness that implied a deep connection that both of us hoped would translate into the real world; lord knows I never saw you nervous in any normal social situation thereafter. I told you it'd be easy to pick me out of a crowd, as I was at the time a strapping young lad at over six feet tall, 230 pounds, shaved head, glasses, and you described yourself as having shoulder-length brown hair, a long flowing skirt, big eyes, and big boobs.

After spending a half-hour staring at the chest of every woman within eyeshot, I caught a glimpse of you crossing the street, and it was all over. I was gone. The idealized image of you I'd created in my head was poured onto concrete and turned into flesh. You had hair like cinnamon and the biggest, most beautiful brown eyes; they seemed to take up your entire face. You also had the warmest and most welcoming smile, and made immediate eye contact with me. It was part of the unique skill you possessed to make everyone around you feel immediately like they were your dearest friend. All of my petty neuroses vanished, and I'd already composed the perfect three-minute pop song in my head for you, one with two separate killer hooks, a devastating bridge, and more melody than the entire Beatles back catalog. I presented you with a cheap and tacky rose I'd purchased at Cumberland Farms as a way to try and ease the anticipated awkwardness, but you seemed genuinely touched by the gesture. It also proved completely unnecessary. You were so outgoing and friendly, and you filled all of the potentially awkward silences with interesting and funny observations and anecdotes.

We went to dinner at NECI Commons. You ordered pasta with pesto (you always ordered the pesto dish) and I ordered meatloaf, which could have been a major mistake—what if you'd been a vegetarian? When getting to know someone, you generally want to avoid extreme opinions, at least initially, and red meat is a pro-life/pro-choice-level extreme. Chicken or fish is generally a much safer choice. ("But it's free-range cow," I envisioned yelling as you ran screaming from the restaurant after my culinary faux pas.)

I spent the evening trying to look at myself through your eyes, to think of things to say that would make myself more appealing to you. I didn't lie or embellish; I merely answered questions and proposed conversation topics that would bring out certain qualities in myself that I felt you would find appealing. We'd already covered so much ground in the emails and phone calls that preceded our migration from the virtual world to the real one, so some of the big ticket items like political leanings—"I'm sort of a socialist," you said, where I was more of a pragmatic liberal—were covered. (Honestly, you could've been a fascist or even a Republican and I still would have loved you.)

We left the restaurant and walked to the Burlington Waterfront. We sat on a swinging bench at the edge of Lake Champlain, and just talked. You told a story about something that had happened at school, a girl being raped and how the school hadn't fulfilled its legal obligation to investigate it. The passion, the stridence, the anger... I felt shallow because you may as well have been giving a dissertation on the mating ritual of the dung beetle. I was too busy observing every gesture, trying to ascertain its significance, while every sentence was analyzed for inflection and context. As soon as you begin looking for signs of attraction, everything the person does or says can be interpreted to mean almost anything. The more signs I looked for from you, the more I found.

At the absolute minimum, I wanted to hold your hand. Here I was, a thirty-year old man... when does this kind of thing end? Without knowing if you were a hand-holder, I was hesitant to make that first move. While walking, I tried to make occasional contact, as if the brush of flesh would make you realize that your dry hand would like a sweaty companion. When you finally took my hand and said you'd come to my apartment, I knew that we would be together both for that night and for the rest of our lives.

We decided to watch a movie. I got us drinks, and we sat on my futon and watched "Grosse Pointe Blank" on DVD. About midway through the movie, around the scene where John Cusack's character gets in a gunfight with his would-be assassin at the Ultramart, we avoided the next major dating quandary—the whole awkward end-of-date "to kiss or not to kiss" issue—by skipping it altogether and having sex.

There was a moment that night when you stopped me and asked if I was sure I wanted to do this, and I looked directly into your eyes and said yes, that I wanted this more than anything I'd ever wanted before. That was the moment, for me, where I knew that we would either find or lose our souls together.

"I don't know anything about sex," I told you.

"You'll be great," you said, and I believed you.

We were in perfect synch that night. We were messy

and noisy and rough and tender and soft as we gorged on each other. We laughed, we held each other, we lied still in the dark and felt our hearts beat in unison. We said goodnight, but were too raw for kisses. You turned over and within seconds were sleeping soundly. Oblivion didn't come for me that night; I'd reached the point where I was so tired, I couldn't sleep at all.

The next morning, you had to leave at seven. I would give you a ride to your friend Kate's house, as she was your ride to the Green Mountain Leadership Expedition, where you would be spending the next week counseling teens who were struggling with bad behavior or grades while fending or encouraging the advances of other horny 20-something counselors. I got out of bed at six and put on a pair of underwear and a T-shirt. The bedroom reeked of sex, that heady combination of sweat and other bodily fluids that we would come to know so well over the next year. I went to the bathroom and stared at myself in the mirror, trying to comprehend what had just happened. It had been nearly five years since I'd even gone on a date, and over a decade since I'd shared a bed with someone. My brain was firing off in every possible direction as I planned out an entire future with you, a person I'd just met for the first time in my life. I was already planning every future conversation, every next step; I had the road to our eventual wedding already mapped out. Fuck spontaneity, right? I was fully committed to not screwing anything up. It wasn't just that I thought you were my last chance for happiness, though it was clearly on my mind. It was that I'd never, in all of my years, experienced anything like the rush I felt the night I met you. I'd waited seemingly forever to be in love, and it was like I'd suddenly swallowed a piece of heaven. The feeling that something was going to change was overwhelming... and it did, everything changed. And I changed too, not right away, but it was the start.

I got back into bed as you stirred awake. You opened your eyes and looked right into mine. I placed my hand on your stomach. "I christen this my belly," I whispered as I pressed my lips upon your warm flesh. I passed over your breasts, making circular motions around your nipples as your breathing started to quicken. I traced the outline of your face with my index finger, starting at the chin and moving along your cheeks, across your forehead, down your nose and over your lips. At that moment, you were the most beautiful thing on this earth.

You asked me what I was thinking about. "I can't believe this happened," is what I said.

"Does it bother you?"

"No. Does it bother you?"

"No."

"Good."

Time stopped as we talked. Everything was good. Everything was perfect.

An hour later, we got dressed and shared the casual laughs and talked the mundane talk of the compatible and the comfortable. It felt like we'd been waking up together for years. There was no time for food or coffee or showers, so we left my apartment with each other's smells all over our bodies. We held hands walking out of my apartment; we held hands in the car on the drive to Kate's apartment. We kissed as you exited my car, and I could see your eyes welling up. What were you feeling? Were you happy? Sad?

You waved to me as I pulled out of the parking lot. I waved back and drove home. I spent the rest of the day exhausted, but my head was buzzing. You told me you'd call me that night from camp, and you did. You called on the next night too. And every other night. You'd squirrel away from the camp to a remote phone and call me collect, and we ended up speaking every night, as there was so much still yet to learn about each other. After three days, I confessed that I'd fallen in love with you, and you cried and said the same thing to me, and I believed you.

I left for England the day before you returned. I had to cover that trade show for music fans, where one could find any manner of brickback for the average Oasis fan. I was there to cover fandom, in general, and specifically fandom for any Vermont-based band with any international following. You were impressed with the opportunity; me, not so much. It was a dumb assignment, since few people in the States had any knowledge of most Vermont-based bands—looking for it overseas was the height of stupid. England wasn't big jam-band territory, outside of a few bands who flirted with the sound, like Stereophonics. Primal Scream tried, but the scenesters value genuineness, and there was never anything genuine about Primal Scream.

As I told you in the email I sent before I left, I've never felt so empty when leaving for such a beautiful place. I rationalized the disinterest in my assignment because I felt I had more important things to attend to. I knew I could ignore the dreary tasks associated with my job; those could be faked, and I was a seriously good faker. I made lists of things to do, and every task, no matter how trivial, was filled with great meaning to me and hopefully to you. I would go around town buying T-shirts, CDs, piles of postcards, a plastic London cab, and a few dozen other useless items, but that wasn't the extent of my plan. At a minimum, I'd planned on calling you every day and on mailing you as many postcards as I could afford. Random ones. Funny ones. Inappropriate ones. I had your phone number and address written down on a sheet of paper, because I hadn't committed either to memory because, well, we'd known each other for a day and all.

The first call came from the Burlington International Airport. I got your voice mail. I doubt you remember the message; I'm not even sure what I said. Probably something profound, like, "Hi, I'm at the airport. Love you. See you when I get back. Good bye." I probably should've invented some amazing romantic language and pretended that I was the suave Romeo, but you know I'm not really that person.

My connecting flight was through Logan Airport in Boston, so it was the location of my second call. I found a pay phone, got ready to call, and realized that I'd left the piece of paper with your number and address at the phone booth in Burlington. My plan was ruined. No phone calls. No postcards. Nothing. I dug into the furthest recesses of my brain looking for your phone number somewhere behind my high school locker combination, but the only one I could come up with was the one I believed was your friend Mike's. I called the number, hoping indeed that it was the right person, and got an anonymous male voice mail. It could have been him, or it could have been any one of thousands of Middlebury students who sounded like stoners. "Uh, this is a friend of a friend... this is Mike... you don't know me but...." Yeah, I never even got that far.

I spent the days in London missing you. I so wanted to take you to all of the places I visited, but we never had the chance. The return flight was the longest I've ever experienced. I had a movie continuously playing on repeat in my head, of me running up to a door, it opening, and... nothing. When it came to the time when you finally opened the door, I'd forgotten what you looked like. This was foolish, right? I felt like I would die if I didn't see you again but wasn't sure if I could've picked you out of a crowd. If I was really in love with you, how could I not remember every part of your face? The reality, of course, is that we'd only spent one night and morning together, but shouldn't you have left a more indelible impression?

I called you the moment I walked in my apartment. It was midnight, but you were still awake at your mother's house in Lyndonville. She wouldn't be back until the following day, so you told me to come over. It was madness; I was jet lagged, but still drove two hours and a hundred miles to be with you that night. It was pitch-black, and the road was blurry. My exhaustion was fighting with my excitement, and winning. The boredom of the highway wasn't making it easier; the deer that ran across Route 2 woke me right up and carried me through to your mom's house.

I ran up to the door, my brain mush, my memory failing, and as soon as you opened the door, everything immediately flooded back. I'll never forget your face that night, the one I'd forgotten after ten days of separation. Your nose was runny, your voice rough, your hair pulled back, your face rosy from the cool air... you, my dear, were a mess that night. You were sick and flu-ish, but you were the person I remembered, the person I loved.

Your eyes teared up. "Why are you crying?" I asked.

"I missed you so much."

"I missed you too."

"I cried the night you left for London."

We hugged some more and sat down on your mom's couch. I gave you postcards and knickknacks, and a book of poems I'd written for you, scribbled on notes throughout the city and transcribed on the flight home into a leather-bound book. They weren't very good, but you acted like it was the most important piece of literature ever written. You flipped through each page and read each one aloud.

"I love you Mike," you said laughing as the tears came again. "I really do." I was going to tell you I loved you too, but before I could you were in my arms and kissing me so hard and deep that I almost fell over. Then I actually fell over, and we rolled on the floor laughing.

I caught my breath. "Does this mean you're my girlfriend?"

"What do you think?"

"I think we were a couple the second we met."

Being with you again was the sweetest of paradoxes, a mix of the familiar and the new. The pieces were falling back into place, yet I still kept pulling away and breaking off kisses to look at you, to take in the new once again. We sat in your childhood bed, my back against the wall and your head on my chest. You became lost in some sort of dreaminess. "This is the end of the line," you said before falling asleep. "We'll never be apart again."

—

Now listening to: "Cinnamon Girl" - Neil Young

Subject: History
From: Mike Norton
To: XXXXXX XXXX

Facebook is an exercise in historical revisionism. We post and tag all of the photos and events of our pasts in order to bathe in their warm, comfortable, rose-scented waters, perpetuating our state of denial over our present miseries.

Despite my own aversion to holding up the past as this idealized time when everything was perfect and awesome and cool and happy and fun and exciting, I'm human. So yes, I imagine what we'd be like today if we'd stayed together. We'd still be a couple, of course. Still married. Still in love. Still laughing at each other's jokes. Still arguing over politics. The idea that we would somehow drift apart, that any of our trivial differences would become Real Serious Issues over time, doesn't really compute.

I imagine the years between then and now being full

of traveling, sitting in bars, going to shows, and listening to music. I imagine weekends spent reading books at bookstores, watching movies, and visiting art exhibits. Long walks, hikes, camping. There are dinner parties, a particularly alien construct the likes of which I've never been in a position to experience, but would participate with the zeal of an anthropologist. I imagine us active politically and socially, with an enormous circle of friends.

We buy organic fair trade local space-grown grass-fed cage-free free-range fruits and vegetables from local Farmers Markets because we want to support our local economies. We eat dinner at home most nights; we've become terrific cooks, eating foods of varying ethnicities, always trying new things. We spend a lot of time thinking about our carbon footprint, about whether to save up money to switch to solar. We drive a Prius, never really doing the calculations on whether the cost of disposing its battery properly offsets its energy savings. If we stay in Vermont, it'll be a Subaru because, yeah, you need a Subaru in Vermont. So cheap! So versatile! So useful!

We shop at thrift stores instead of big box stores, we go to garage sales and antique shops. We walk, we bike, we compost, we have "unplug" weeks. We have a small circle of extremely close friends, and we spend a lot of time with them going to movies, art exhibits, sitting in cafes discussing issues. We have straight and gay couple friends, and we're the bedrock pair that they all aspire to be, and we help everyone through the messiness of relationship maintenance because we are the pros at this. We watch very little TV and listen to NPR, or whatever music we've discussed. We share chores. We sit in bed together, you knitting or doing something crafty or creative while I play with my laptop. We read Utne Reader, McSweeney's, Huffington Post, Talking Points Memo, and God knows what other publications religiously. We browse Etsy religiously. Sexism and homophobia and racism and Republicans easily offend us, and we're quick to judge white people from the Midwest or the South.

We are happy, and then we are pregnant, and then everything changes.

I imagine our daughter—it's always a girl for some reason—being eight years old right now. We're raising her in Portland or Seattle or Austin or Madison or Burlington, some interesting and ideally ethnically diverse city that isn't too big or small, has good schools, progressive political views, lots of expensive sandwich shops, and a vibrant art scene.

We spend our days working. You're running a non-profit or some other social program, doing Very Important Work saving the planet or humanity or both. I'm a full-time paid blogger, writing about things of little consequence but getting paid handsomely to do so and using what little free time I have to do important volunteer work at your job. I'm a stay-at-home dad, and I take our extremely gifted child to an extremely diverse gifted school every day. While she's at school, I work. When she gets home, I help her with her homework and spend as much time as possible encouraging her various creative endeavors. When you come home, you pick up where I leave off, delighting in her creations and creating mini-installations in our cozy house for each like they're works of fine art.

We are happy and we are content and we are a family.

We sound like the most stereotypical white yuppie/hippie couple imaginable, not too far removed from people like Bain. By all rights, I should hate us but I don't because I realize that the bile I direct at those kinds of people is just jealousy over lives and lifestyles I will never experience.

—

Now listening to: "Marry Me" - St. Vincent

CHAPTER SEVEN

I walked ahead of Bain, the temptation growing within me to put this sad evening behind me and bolt for my apartment. If I had to guess, I'd say Bain would've caught up to me about half a block down the street, particularly since I'd already be coughing up a lung.

"Mike, wait up," Bain said.

"What?" I said, stopping and turning around.

"I'm sorry about what happened in there."

"Don't sweat it," I said. An alchoholiday was sounding pretty fabulous at the moment. "Square Pegs is just up the street a bit."

"I was being a bit of a dick," he said.

Yes, he was being a bit of a dick. Or maybe he wasn't; I'll leave that up to you to decide. You'll probably pick his side. Everyone does. "You weren't being a dick," I said. "It's okay. It's cool."

"I was just trying to make some small talk, and bring both of us up to speed on where we're at," he said, and for a moment he was the old Bain. "We used to talk about things for hours, and constantly make fun of each other."

"I know, it's just been a tough year."

"I hear you. It's tough for everyone."

"Yeah, I guess so," I said, knowing the two of us weren't on the same page. "But you're all married with kids."

"I know, right?" Bain said, clearly proud. "It's crazy."

"I never saw that one coming."

"I feel like I'm still the same guy, just in a nicer suit, you know?"

"How did you swing it?" I asked. "How'd you make the transition to being a grown up?"

"You have to be willing to let things go, to release them into the wild, like a rehabilitated sea lion or a starlet."

"You have to Lohan it?"

"Exactly."

We both laughed. He was trying to be a decent and respectful human being, so I figured the least I could do is allow him to pity me.

"So why aren't you married, Mr. Norton?" he asked.

"Oh God no...."

"Come on," he laughed. "It's what all the cool kids are doing nowadays. You're smart, you're funny. Why isn't there a wife and 2.5 kids waiting for you at home?"

It's a reasonable perfectly question. You may have gathered that it's one I'm a wee-bit obsessed with, almost as much as I'm obsessed with Facebook. The topic of marriage comes up a lot, mostly when I speak with people in the "older than me" category. They ask a series of leading questions to ascertain my marital status, poking and prodding as they try to figure out whether this particular sad-sack forty-year-old is divorced, tragically widowed, possibly gay and lonely, or perhaps most salaciously, all of the above. I always lie and tell them no, that I'm not currently married, nor have I never been married because I don't want to be that guy who tells that one sad tale of a past love over and over. You know that guy, right? You hate that guy. I'm that guy and I hate that guy.

When it came to discussing the topic with Bain, I went through the usual pat answers, memorized from years of repetition and performances: I haven't met the right woman, I'm in no rush, I enjoy my life, blah blah blah. What I should've said is no, it won't happen (again), not on a bet, that I'd rather scrub my tongue with a piece of sandpaper than walk down the aisle (again). But I can't be that cynical. I still entertain the quaint notion that I'll meet another woman of my dreams, or at least a person who'll be willing to settle for me. I need a woman who sees a lack of ambition and a tendency toward laziness not as fatal character flaws but as highly desirable attributes, the sort of older woman who's desperate, has low expectations, and a mortal fear of dying alone and unmarried. That's the only kind of woman who'd have any interest in someone like me, and God knows, that sounds like a horrible, horrible person.

Bain's response to my pat answer was typical, telling me that it must be awesome to be single, that it's the greatest thing in the world. I'm unattached, free to womanize and pursue the exotic. As I rapidly approach middle age, I've come to realize that that it's impossible to live that idealized single lifestyle unless you're famous or wealthy. Married men bitch about the frequency of sex with their wives, or its lack thereof, but what about the celibacy that occurs when you're single? There's a quiet desperation people feel when they have no companionship, no one to share their lives with, no prospects on the horizon, nothing to eat in the fridge, and have extended periods without sex. At least those married men get to be celibate for a reason, even if it makes them resent their wives and rationalize their pursuit of twenty-one-year-old interns.

For us single people who aren't sleeping around, it's just a long, empty moment. A horny one too, but that sort of goes without saying.

—

Now listening to: "We End Up Together" - The New Pornographers

Subject: All of My Days
From: Mike Norton
To: XXXXXX XXXX

There's one other memory that I walk through over and over again, much like our first date. It starts with a simple question from me: "How'd you sleep?"

"Like a baby," you whispered into my ear. "I was exhausted after our workout last night."

"No kidding," I leaned back and placed my arms over my head. "I was fantastic."

You snorted. "Yeah, right."

"What can I say?"

"Not that much, Skippy, not that much at all."

"Ooh, I love it when you call me Skippy," I said as I pulled you towards me. "It makes me feel all macho and sexy."

I suppose that little voice in the back of my head was always there, saying "something bad will happen." And sure enough, you broke out the three words no one ever wants to hear while lazily lounging around on a Sunday morning: "We need to talk."

I could feel all of my confidence melting away. I started sweating.

"Okay, let's talk."

"I've been doing some thinking the last few weeks, about grad school and degrees, and I've found a title I want more than doctor."

"Really? Like what. President? Prime Minister? Nobel Prize Winner. God?"

You briefly looked down, collecting your thoughts. After an excruciating pause, you looked directly into my eyes and bored a hole directly into my soul. "Mother."

"Ah yes, that is the big title, isn't it?"

"Probably the biggest," you said as you stood up and walked to the kitchen. I followed. "Like I said, I've been doing a lot of thinking."

I put my arms around your waist. "Today, standing here behind you, in this oh-so-luxurious apartment that we share together" I whispered in your ear. "I know I want to be a father."

"Really," you said turning around. "I thought that if I mentioned this to you, you'd say 'gotta go' and be out of the room."

"Why would I do that?" I said as I backed away a step.

"I don't know. Boys are like that."

"Well, I'm not like most boys."

"No kidding."

"I guess it's part of getting older," I said. "All of the things you used to dismiss become easier to consider."

"I don't know anything about that myself," you said with a sly grin. "But I've been thinking a lot. And I know it is important to me."

I've always had strange issues with parenting. I could say, and have said, I didn't want to have kids. It's practically unnatural to find conversations about babies boring, and there's always some point in your childless thirties when breeders' constant talk about how lucky you are not to have children tying you down or how you can head off on a moment's notice to some far-flung destination begins feeling patronizing. It's like it's the consolation prize, but they secretly know their life is richer and more rewarding. That biological clock is, after all, always ticking away. My own reality has always been slightly different. It's true to say that there were various times of my life where I couldn't see myself with a child; however, I always assumed I would when it made sense.

I carefully chose my words. "Starting a family makes sense when you're with the person you want to spend your life with." I placed my arms around your waist, moved your hair to the side and gently kissed you on the back of her neck.

You broke free from my grasp, and quickly wiped a tear away from your face. "Will you love me when I'm fat?" you asked, pausing to look at your midsection. "Or at least fatter."

"I'll love you even if you balloon up to three-hundred pounds."

"Is that the limit?"

"I'm afraid so."

"Then I better get started."

You looked disapprovingly at the clutter in our bedroom and sighed. It was all of my stuff flung around the room, shirts on the floor, shoes in the middle of the room, socks stuck in them. The laundry basket stuffed full of dirty clothes in the corner. You removed the towel from your head and sat down on our unmade bed. "This place is a mess," you said.

"Awl," I said. "Do you really want to fight now, after this special moment?"

You leaned over and kissed me on the lips. "Of course not, handsome. This room is in perfect shape."

"That's more like it," I said. "Mmm, your hair smells good." I always loved the smell of your hair.

"I'm thinking of cutting it off," you said.

"Don't you ever do it," I said. "It might contain all of your superhuman strength."

"True," you said. You rubbed my bald head. "Good thing yours is stored elsewhere."

"Yes, in my pants."

"God, you're such a dork," you said. You began to comb your hair with the brush you bought at the .99 cent store. "I don't know why I love you."

"What does that say about you, loving a dork and all."

"I'll have to ask my shrink. She has all the answers."

"I bet she does," I said, frowning slightly at the small crack in the ceiling of our apartment. "So what are we going to do on this fine Sunday?"

"Not much, not much at all."

You looked at your reflection in the living room mirror, rubbed your eyes, and slowly and deliberately placed the brush down on the end table. "What are you doing for the next fifty years?" you asked without turning around.

"Let me go check my Outlook calendar."

"Forget it."

"To answer your question, I plan on spending the next fifty years with you."

"Is that right?" You untangled your hair with your fingers. "Is that some sort of proposal or something?"

"It's something better," I said. "It's a promise."

You turned around, your eyes enormous and radiant. "Let's get married," you said.

"Okay."

"As soon as possible."

"How about next week?"

"Okay."

"Okay."

I don't think either of us knew what to say at this point, so we just held each other for minutes or hours or days.

"How about those Red Sox?" you said pulling away. I smiled. A few days later—eight days that are a complete blur, to be specific—we were married in a civil ceremony in Burlington.

Why did we do it this way? Why didn't we have a traditional wedding and reception? Is that what you really wanted? Should I have pressed you to have a bigger ceremony, to make it out to be a more important event? You mother seemed disappointed, though she claimed to understand. For me, it was incredibly good news. I was worried about who I'd invite. With both of my parents long gone and my sister being too poor to attend even if she knew or cared about it, I'd have no blood representation. Would I invite co-workers? They were more like acquaintances than close friends. Maybe they had some idea I was in better-than-normal spirits for the last year, that there was some sort of spring in my step or that dating glow people have when in a relationship— that sudden realization that they can now freely talk to people without worrying about flirting—but they weren't the kind of people I'd consider inviting to such a private event.

The ceremony was simple and fast. There was a judge, a formal and legally-binding message, a pair of "I dos," the exchange of our cheap thrift store rings that cost us a grand total of a hundred bucks, and we were done. In and out in a couple of hours. You wore your favorite dress, I wore my only dress pants and a new tie. We kissed, gently at first, our fingers entwined. I pulled back. "If we don't stop this soon, they're going to ask us to leave," I said.

"Let go, dumbass," you said as you tried to release your hands, but my grip on you only got tighter. "If you don't let me go we can't leave and go have sex."

We returned to our apartment, but I told you to wait before you opened the door. "You're not carrying me in," you said.

"No, I'm not."

Instead, I blindfolded you. "What's this all about?" you asked.

"Wait and see," I said. I opened the door and guided you in, past the clutter in the living room. I stopped in the doorway of the bedroom. "Ready?"

"Yes, yes, what is it?"

I removed the blindfold. In the bedroom, in place of the much-maligned futon we'd been sleeping on for the previous year, was a new queen-sized bed that I'd paid a lot of money to have delivered that day. You shrieked and leaped onto it.

"It's amazing," you said as you bounced up and down. You flopped onto your stomach. "Just perfect. How could you afford this?"

"I had some savings," I lied, as I'd just charged it all to a credit card you didn't know about. "It was on sale."

"You didn't have to, you know... I mean, not just for me."

"I know."

"This is just outstanding," you said. "Because it is all about my needs, right?"

"Of course. I just get sex as payment."

"You're so crude."

"You like me when I'm crude."

"No, I do not."

"Sure you do." I fell on top of you and started to remove your clothes. "Besides, I learned all of those crude words from you."

"You need to pay for being so crude."

"Since when is that a crime? What's the penalty?"

"You'll have to fuck the living daylights out of me right now."

Five hours and multiple bottles of cheap champagne later, we drunkenly stared at the ceiling in our new bed. "Did we really do this?" you asked.

"I think so."

"Can we really handle this?"

"I think so."

You put your head down on the pillow and fell asleep. I couldn't take my eyes off you because I was afraid you might disappear during the night.

—

Now listening to: "All Of My Days And All Of My Days Off" - A.C. Newman

Subject: Squared Up
From: Mike Norton
To: XXXXXX XXXX

By the time Bain and I arrived at Square Pegs, there was a short line outside the bar. What had started as a gentle, pulsating thump from a distance had turned into a cacophony of crap as we stood with the hipster twenty-somethings waiting to enter the bar. According to a sign outside, someone named DJ Nastee—who was surely making his parents, Mr. and Mrs. Nastee, proud—was spinning reggae and ska and dancehall and apparently some of the worst music known to man and God, and he was doing it at ear-splitting volume. Looking at all of the pretty people standing around, I realized that I should've worn nicer pants. That alone would've given me the confidence to walk confidently through a place like this. My second thought was that I wish I had earplugs. My third thought was that I wish I was anywhere else, like maybe Afghanistan, though I'm not sure its music would be any less annoying.

The bouncer gave Bain and I a free pass on the ID check at the door, which was moderately depressing. Upon entry, I was immediately struck the horribleness of the place, the people, the music, and the atmosphere. The walls were a particularly lurid shade of red, the rest a mix of blacks and blackers and blackests. The crowd spilled out of the bar and into the cordoned-off side alley; it was exclusively young, white, confident, ironically attired, foolish, skinny, sullen, pierced, bejeweled, and dreadlocked. All of the people at the place were iconoclasts, despite their obvious conformity. The bar area smelled like AXE and Chlamydia.

"This is my kind of place," Bain said, giving the place a quick once-over. I scanned the room for someone who looked more desperate and out-of-place than I did, and failed.

"What'll you have?" the bartender screamed at Bain.

"Give me a shot of Talisker 10, neat."

"I'll have that too," I said, even though I had no idea what I was ordering. I've stopped drinking because I don't like to do it alone. Bars are even more insufferable than normal when you're sober.

"Man," Bain said as we nursed our drinks, "that's some peaty goodness."

I gulped it down in one shot, burning my throat, stomach, and possibly lower intestine. "Oh yeah, me too," is what I think I said.

We grabbed another drink and found a table near the door. The skies parted and cried "Hallelujah" as Mr. Nastee finished his set and took a methamphetamine and ketamine break. With no music to drown out the crowd, the sounds of hipsters trying to out-apathy each other became even more insufferable. Each conversation, more mundane and inane than the other, made me want to gouge out my eardrums with one of the tendrils from DJ Nastee's dreadlocks.

"God, there are women everywhere," Bain said.

"Yeah," I said, realizing that there was no one within eyeshot that was remotely attractive to me. Or I should say, they were all attractive in the way that strippers and Sarah Palin are attractive, but not exactly my type.

"You know what?" Bain said?

I didn't really want to know. "What?"

"I'm going to get you laid tonight," he said, his face lighting up like he'd just won the lottery. "That'll perk up that sour mood of yours."

"Dude, seriously?"

Bain pressed me. "Seriously," he said. He seemed to wait for a reaction, something, anything. "Okay, fine. What's the real story? Someone break your heart?"

How was I supposed to respond? Should I have divulged the details of our sad little story? Would telling him everything make him understand, and did I even care if he got it or not?

"That's it," Bain continued, increasing his level of smugness into the realm of dickheadedness as he leaned back in his chair. "Some little chica broke your little heart?"

—

Now listening to: "Broken Heart" - Spiritualized

Subject: Broken
From: Mike Norton
To: XXXXXX XXXX

Yes, some little chica broke my little heart. Yes, I've never recovered. Yes, I've spent years spiraling down some dark path to an uncertain final destination.

These are the truths I couldn't tell him, or to anyone else. Each year I've grown more accustomed to your absence, more tolerant to the pain, but it's inaccurate to say that I've gotten past it. In fact, it has defined every single minute of my life since the day you left. I'm not sure if you want to hear about some of the debauchery that took place. It's not the fun kinds that involve drugs, banging twins in trashed hotel rooms, or Tarantino-esque tales of drug buys gone awry. Instead, it's sad, pathetic tales of drinking alone, vomiting in the bathroom, of going weeks without washing.

I wish I could say that I spent those first few weeks in

bed sobbing until my eyes stopped generating tears and my throat was raw from wailing, but that was never in the cards. I've never once been able to cry over the loss of what I'd like to think was once us. Instead, I took some time off from work to have a nervous breakdown. Every morning it was like there was a ten-ton weight on my chest, that daily realization that nothing was the same as it was previously, and it would never be the same again. I slept a lot. I rarely got out of bed. I drank so I'd pass out and not dream. I didn't answer the phone. When I did crawl out of bed, I'd look in the mirror and see someone who looks not entirely like me. He had similar features, for sure, but he was an imposter, a stand-in. He had hollowed out eyes, even less hair, and his face was redder and puffier.

Eventually, I grew tired of the bed and performed a ritualistic cleansing of our apartment. I swept the wood floors and scrubbed the bathroom. I carefully removed the cushions from our couch, looking for anything of yours that slipped through the cracks; after staring at it for a day, I sold it for fifty bucks to some college kids because I wasn't sure I could ever get you out of it. I also gave away our mattress; that was an easy call. Your mother came by. I guess that was easier, right? She had little to say to me, and slowly and methodically placed the rest of your things into boxes and walked them out to her car. Your sister called twice, and she sounded so much like you on the phone that by the end of the conversations, I was dripping with sweat and unable to respond. She made one trip to our apartment and looked exactly like a 17-year old version of you. It was more than I could bear.

A few of our shared friends tried to drop by or call, to

make attempts at bringing me up from the bottom of the depths. They offered up their condolences, discussed their own similar experiences with loss, delivered their pithy "things will get better" anecdotes, and they kept expecting things to get better. Independently, they all came to the realization that things weren't getting better, and that I didn't want to get better; I am, if anything, stubborn and persistent in both happiness and misery. Over time, they stopped calling or checking in altogether. I couldn't blame them for letting me be, really. I was swimming in a sea of despair, and unless they were willing to risk drowning with me, they were better off watching me flail away from the safety of the shore. Still, I wish they'd tried harder because sometimes you just want them to call, even when you don't want to talk to them.

I returned to my job but wasn't exactly doing my best work. I was showing up late, and when I was there I really wasn't there. I came to work drunk a few times, and people looked at me like I was an alien and treated me like an infant. They'd ask if I was okay, and I'd tell them I was fine. They'd ask if there was anything they could get for me, or do for me, and I'd tell them that no, I was fine. It was like that song "Institutionalized" by Suicidal Tendencies, which you've probably never heard of because it was released before you were born. Mike Muir just wanted a Pepsi and his mom wouldn't give it to him, believing instead that he was on drugs and in need of therapy. All I wanted was to be left alone, so I wrote a column about how the Burlington music scene was garbage, laying out in excruciating detail how terrible I found Phish and all of the band members' various side projects. It was perhaps my finest work, a three-thousand-word missive that was full of strong language, graphic violence, and full-frontal nudity. My editor, an incredibly generous and patient guy named Dan who deserved much better, said that perhaps I should take more time off and consider working at home. I couldn't figure out why he wanted me to stay. I quit on the spot.

(To this day, Dan occasionally sends me flattering e-mails asking me if I'd be interested in contributing to the paper's website. A part of me still wants to write about music, but only if I come across something I really like or that I feel genuinely passionate about in some way. As I've gotten older, it's become more and more difficult to keep up with any scene. Spending nights in smoke-filled clubs or weekends at smelly and uncomfortable festivals is for the young. I barely have the energy and desire to keep up with all of the fanzines and blogs devoted to discovering new and interesting music. It's not a matter of loving music any less; if anything, I'm more capable of being more passionate about certain bands or songs today than I ever was when I pursuing everything. I'm simply less curious than I used to be, and my tastes and interests have narrowed considerably.)

I spent six months living off my limited savings and whatever I could sell, including the SAAB that you loved so much. I got a couple grand for it, which was a few thousand less than expected because it blew a head gasket. It wasn't like I could afford to fix it, so the mechanic made me a deal and probably flipped it for like six grand. Whatever, I had a bit more scratch to let me pay rent for another three months.

I charged things on credit cards and paid the minimum. My debt went up over twenty thousand bucks because I was buying things that I hoped would bring some degree of happiness. While they didn't brighten my mood any, they brought convenience. They brought a clearer HD picture. They brought more storage for my Tivo. They brought better graphics for my videogames. These suddenly seemed like important things, especially when I wasn't leaving my apartment for weeks on end. I got heavily invested in Internet relationships. It was perfect. There was no physical connection, just chatrooms. I dated these exotic and beautiful online creatures, for a mere $4.99 a minute. I even took one of those chatroom romances into the real world, or at least the non-paying virtual world. She was a random girl, possibly from South Carolina. We messaged each other for hours every day, talking about the mundane details of our lives. We flirted. We talked about getting together some day. We shared. We connected. I decided I had to meet her in person and flew to Charleston, but couldn't leave the airport. I didn't want to know if she was telling me the truth about herself or if she was just the role-playing character of a fat, sweaty, bald forty-year-old. Maybe he got up to level sixty when my plane landed.

I returned to Burlington, out of money and manic. I couldn't figure out what to do with my hands; they'd just flap about at my sides or in front of me. I wanted to talk to you, I needed to talk to you, but that wasn't possible. There was no one around, but it didn't really matter; I was muted. I lacked the vocabulary to handle the kind of Real Loss that doesn't go away. It stared me right in the face and rendered me speechless. You'd think I would've been prepared. It's not like I hadn't always imagined what Real Loss really meant. I'd crafted detailed scenarios in my head where I face real unimaginable Real Loss with bravery and tragic grandeur, emerging afterward even stronger and more grounded. The reality proved quite different. Real Loss just made me stupid and pathetic and sad, with nothing to look forward to but an occasional TV show, Internet porn, and alcohol. Each offered the relief of the dead, disconnected from real human emotions.

You were everywhere, in the air and water, in the light and in the dark. I could still smell your skin after a shower, hear the rumble of your stomach when hungry and the sound of a brush passing through your hair, feel the calluses on your fingers, see the shape of your eyes when you awakened. I tried to get over you. I tried to forget you. I tried to wash you off me, I tried to drink you away. I tried to clear you out of memory, delete you from my history. I called you, I left you e-mails, I drove to places I thought you'd be. You were nowhere. You'd evaporated. You left me behind. I was wrecked. We were married, and then we weren't married. All of the delight I derived from the world was gone. Did you have to do it? Why did you do it? I miss you so much.

—

Now listening to: "Holocaust" - Big Star

CHAPTER EIGHT

As the evening wore on, the air got heavier with smugness and thicker with irony, leaving me hacking and wheezing like I'd swallowed a cat.

Bain and I were on our fourth or fifth round of drinks, jumping between whiskey and martinis, and I'd already lost count of the number of times I was disgusted and/or in awe of his ability to be simultaneously horrible and interesting. At some point, Bain had struck up a conversation with three women, all tall and thin and blonde and freckled and high-cheekboned and insane and named Amber or Ashley or some other stripper name. He treated the corner of the bar like it was his house, draping his arms over the edge of the booth and around the girls. Our server, who was also named Amber or Ashley or something, had apologized profusely for not being her usual bubbly self because she'd only gotten up a couple of hours earlier after taking pure MDMA instead of her usual Ecstasy. I guess Monday is a big party night in Burlington.

"What do they normally use to cut your E?" Bain asked her.

"What?"

"Does it have meth in it? Caffeine? Dextromethorphan? Ephedrine? Coke?"

"They put coke in E?" Ashley/Amber 2 asked.

"I've never heard of that," Ashley/Amber 1 said.

"Oh yeah," Bain said. "I spent one weekend doing like a quarter of an eightball, and then someone broke out the E and we did a couple of rolls, and like holy shit I was flying. After the second bump, I was buzzing."

I had no idea what he was talking about.

"You ever do any candy flipping?" Ashley/Amber 2 said.

"Never heard of it," said Bain.

"It's E and LSD."

"Wicked," said Server Ashley/Amber between yawns.

"It's legendary."

"Another round of martinis here," Bain said to Server Ashley/Amber. "Extra dirty for these two."

They giggled. "We're not dirty at all," Ashley/Amber 3 said. "We took showers before we came here tonight."

"Alone?" Bain said.

"Of course, silly," Ashley/Amber 1 said. "But I do like showering with my boyfriends."

"Oh, I don't like that at all," Ashley/Amber 2 said. "Guys always expect me to give them head in the shower because they're so clean."

"Think of the positives of showering with a guy," Bain

said. "At least your tits will be extremely clean."

All three Ashley/Ambers laughed. I coughed up a furball. Bain was soaking it in, and started to clap. Wasn't their laughing already validating his joke? The clapping seemed superfluous.

The extra noise drew the attention of a college-age girl sitting across the room within my eye view. She was staring at me, taking in everything about me, memorizing every freckle, every blotch in my less-than-perfect skin. I'm not a big eye contact person to begin with, and she was making me uncomfortable. I looked back at the bottom of my glass, trying to appear like I was taking part in the conversation going on around me.

"We haven't really spent much time talking about my friend Mike here," Bain said. "He's a famous novelist."

"Oh really?" Ashley/Amber 2 said.

"What?" I said.

Not this again. I decided to play along, though I wondered if this would even be interesting or impressive to anyone nowadays. Seriously, no one sets out to write a book anymore. We're all too busy writing blogs, texting, Tweeting, and whatever new way we digitally express our narcissism. Maybe someone gets a book deal to publish their blog entries or amusing Tweets, or a movie deal based on the book of their blog entries and amusing Tweets. The only people really working on novels are characters in novels, created by lazy writers who use it as shorthand to express the depth of their characters and to put the reader in the head of the author.

Bain cut me off. "No really, he's got a book coming out."

"That's cool," Ashley/Amber 2 said.

"I want to write a book like 'Eat, Pray, Love' some

day," Ashley/Amber 3 said.

"I never would've guessed you were a writer," Ashley/Amber 2 said.

"What's a writer like?" I asked.

"More like, I don't know, bookish?"

"What's the book called?" Ashley/Amber 1 asked.

"Matadors."

"Is it about bullfighting?" Ashley/Amber 3 asked.

"No, it's not about bullfighting."

"Then why's it called Matadors?"

"It's a nickname of the college parts of the book take place in."

"I'm not sure that's a good name," Ashley/Amber 1 said.

"What's it about?" Ashley/Amber 2 said.

"It's about... I don't know, things from my life."

"But it sounds like it's a bio of a bullfighter," Ashley/Amber 1. "You should really think about giving it a better name."

"Thanks, I will."

"When's it's coming out?" Ashley/Amber 2 asked.

I decided to be honest. "Sometime after I've written it."

"I don't get it" Ashley/Amber 3 said. "He said it was coming out."

"Okay, question time," Bain interrupted. "Does size matter?"

"Oh god, yes," said Ashley/Amber 2.

"I went out with this one dude, whoa," Ashley/Amber 1 said. "He was a total cervix banger."

"What the hell is that?" Bain asked.

"He had a giant cock... wait, is this going to bug you?"

"No, go right ahead."

"It wasn't that good. It was totally skinny and long."

"You have to have some girth," said Ashley/Amber 2.

"You also have to be able to last," said Ashley/Amber 3.

"Though not too long," said Ashley/Amber 2.

"Oh god yeah, some guys think fucking like porn stars for hours is actually fun," said Ashley/Amber 1. "I get bored after a while."

"I may not be good, but at least I'm fast," I said.

Ashley/Amber 2 laughed.

"You a one-pump chump, Mr. Writer?" Ashley/Amber 3 said.

Everyone laughed.

"Okay, here's another question for you girls," Bain said. "When you give blow jobs are you a deep throater or a tip nibbler."

"Just the tip," Ashley/Amber 2 said. "My gag reflex is too strong."

"I can't wait to get married so I can stop giving head," Ashley/Amber 1 said.

"Only birthdays, right?" Ashley/Amber 3 said.

"Is that true, Mr. Writer?" Ashley/Amber 2 said. "That when you're married, you never get blowjobs anymore?"

"Don't ask me," I said and pointed at Bain. "Ask him."

"You're married?" Ashley/Amber 3 said.

"You're a funny guy, Mike," Bain said flashing me a violent look, like he wanted to disembowel me on the spot.

"Ladies, it's time for a pee break," Ashley/Amber 1 said.

"Don't take too long," Bain said. "We don't want to have to send a search party out for you."

—

Now listening to: "Drunk Girls" - LCD Soundsystem

Subject: RE: Drunk Girls (2/2)
From: Mike Norton
To: XXXXXX XXXX

Bain's features hardened, his neck grew taut. He had an "I smell poop" look as he crinkled his nose and launched into me. "What's your fucking problem?"

"Why are you yelling at me?" I whined in response.

"You told them I'm married."

"Sorry, man," I said. "It slipped. I'm not used to playing these kinds of games."

"Look, I'm going to fuck someone tonight, and I don't want you to get in my way."

"Then why am I even here?"

"What's your problem?"

"What's my problem? What's your problem with..." I stumbled trying to find something clever. "... what's your problem with my problem?" My problem is that I had no real desire to assist someone in adultery. Not that I'm completely opposed to what he was trying to do; he's an adult, his wife is an adult. If Bain is willing to risk his entire marriage for a one night stand with a post-collegiate bimbo, and this makes the assumption that his wife cares one way or the other, who am I to judge? Still, without knowing his wife's view of all of this, I can't help but put myself in her shoes if this girl ends up going psycho and trying to get hold of him in Los Angeles. It's not like it's particularly hard to track down people nowadays, thanks to websites like... wait for it... Facebook. If his wife does care, ugh. And what about his kid?

"We used to like to go out and drink," Bain said. "We used to have fun hanging out, talking to people. For one night, try to be the guy you used to be before...." He pointed at me with a palpable sense of disgust, which is a pretty tough thing to pull off. "... all of this."

"All of what?"

"Look at you... you're a mess."

I was getting even more pissed. "People who think they have their shit together are delusional... it's like...."

"Stop," Bain interrupted me. "What makes you happy?"

"What makes me happy?" I repeated his quest. Without pause, I launched into a brilliant answer. "Lots of things."

"You're miserable."

"I am not miserable."

"I hate to be the one to say this, but you reek of failure."

I laughed. I couldn't believe I was having this conversation, with Bain of all people. "And you can tell this after a few hours?"

"Yeah, I can," Bain said. "For fuck's sake, get over high

school, get over college, get over whatever it is you're carrying around." He looked me directly in the eye and threw up his arms. "You've given up, man."

He's right. I have given up. It's not the first time. I gave up when started junior high at the ripe old age of thirteen. That period of given up-ness lasted until I got to college, where I emerged from my shell for a few minutes, surveyed the scene, and immediately retreated back inside for the next decade.

Here's the thing. I peaked socially in the fifth grade. Kids always looked up to me. I was actually upset over not winning "Most Popular" in some random school contest. I had two girlfriends that year, Mara Markov, who was Russian and pretty, and with whom I made out frequently. (Where "making out" consisted of kissing in the most awkward manner that an 11-year-old could manage.) I broke up with her when a kid named Nassar Haddad said she was weird looking. I also went out with my neighbor, who was a beautiful Hawaiian girl named Jenny Kealoha. We walked to school together every day, but broke up when she went to a different Junior High School.

I stopped talking to girls at that point, at least until Helen Ramirez awkwardly stumbled into my path. As dark as I am pale, she was exotic and beautiful and Bolivian. We'd known each other for years, but at some point her gawky adolescent nerdiness turned into shapely womanly sexiness. It may have been the weight loss or the contacts, but whatever the cause, our friendship turned into something more substantial. We spent a summer making out in every room of both of our houses, and getting closer and closer to actually having sex. The closer we got, the more terrified I became. After one session of what the instructional films call "mutual masturbation"—an appropriate substitute for full-blown sexual intercourse, they say—I had to break up with her. It wasn't a case of using her and moving on; I was angry because she had the audacity to do these terrible and dirty things with me. And because she was willing to do these things with me, clearly she was willing to do them with anyone. Because really, who was I? I was nobody. I was nothing. At that particular point in my life, I could only view someone who would actually have sex with me with utter disdain. I then spent the next twelve years obsessing over that moment. There were times when I was so naive that I believed I'd done her some sort of harm, that I'd probably turned her into some sort of slut who was fucking everyone and everything or a nun who was unable to look any man in the eyes again. There was no middle ground. Yes, I'm an idiot. We reconnected a few years ago, and of course she was perfectly normal; as if I could ever have that sort of impact on anyone.

Still, the damage was done. I retreated into the life of the hopeless romantic, prone to grand gestures and a complete inability to articulate them to anyone. I was the type who fell in love easily and deeply and frequently. While everyone else was going through the terror and joys of their first crushes, first dates, first kisses, and first boobs, I was falling in love with all of the girls who were ignoring me or dating those feathered-haired Aryan assholes who treated everyone like shit. When those girls broke up with their future husbands I'd be relieved, but nothing would change. I'd still sit in the back of the room dreaming and pining, secretly treasuring and over-analyzing even the briefest encounter. A simple "hi" in a hallway became the most meaningful moment in my life up to that point. The girls, they'd move from one Aryan asshole to another, and never once would I enter their crosshairs. The unreciprocated love, longing, desire, and lust that I directed at any and every girl in vicinity without regard to looks, age, and availability broke my heart every single day.

—

Now listening to: "Devil With The Green Eyes" - Matthew Sweet

Subject: Adults
From: Mike Norton
To: XXXXXX XXXX

I wanted to punch Bain in the face. For being Bain, for making me go out, for making me relive all of this. Who was he to judge me in such a small amount of time? Me, a loser? Someone who's given up? Whether he was right or not wasn't the point; he had no right to act all superior and high and mighty.

"You're one to talk," I spat at him. "You're trying to relive your youth, and pick up these girls… they're children, and possibly retarded."

"So what?" he said.

"What do they get out of it?"

"Who the fuck cares?"

"I live here, I have to see these people."

"I somehow doubt you cross social paths with these girls that often."

I mumbled something profound like, "um... Well... I... um..."

"I could be wrong, though," he said.

He was right. I'd never see these girls again. Maybe we'd walk by each other as they were leaving Banana Republic, and maybe there'd be a flash of "You look familiar" in their faces, though not enough for them to consider stopping and talking. And if I initiated some social interaction, that would redefine awkward. "Hi there!" I'd say, my face all lit up like I'd just run across my best friend in the whole wide world.

"Uh... Hi?" Ashley/Amber would say, as her face moves quickly from shopping bliss to social horror.

"We met at Square Pegs," I'd say. "Spent a few hours talking."

For one or two seconds, I'd feel like the kind of person who socializes with people like this. People would see us talking, women would immediately assume I was more interesting than I look, men would be jealous. I'd be king of the shopping mall.

"Right... Yeah... I'm late for... something..." She'd say, backing slowly away. "Nice seeing you." And then poof, she'd walk away as quickly as possible, something between power walking and a full sprint. She'd turn to her friend, some other member of her Ashley/Amber tribe, and they'd both laugh.

"People in the real world do this all the time," Bain said. "You're overthinking it."

I got all self-righteous. "At least one of us is thinking...." I paused for the pièce de résistance. "... with his brain." Satisfied with my cleverness, I waited for it to register.

Nope, nothing. Didn't register at all.

"I don't need to lie to get into some girl's panties," Bain said, channeling his outermost douchebag.

"But you're not telling them you're married."

"I'm omitting some things, but not lying."

He wins on a technicality.

"Look, these girls aren't innocent," Bain said. "For all I know, they have boyfriends or husbands. I don't care."

"Maybe you should."

Bain leaned back in his chair. "If they don't care, why should I care?" He took a drink and laughed. "Dude, seriously. You need to relax."

"I'm working on it."

"Not hard enough."

We could see the girls exiting the bathroom. One of them waved at Bain as they slithered through the crowd. "If these lovely ladies want to spend a night of fun with me," he said. "Who would I be to stop them?"

"So you're ribbed for their pleasure?"

"Yes, I'm ribbed for their pleasure." Bain picked up his glass triumphantly. "And after this," he poured the last of it down his throat, a drink with an exotic name and a lot of alcohol. "I'll be properly lubricated too."

The girls sat down in some new seating arrangement that was probably designed and debated in the safety of the toilet. It confused me, as I was only able to tell who was who based on proximity.

Bain turned to Ashley/Amber 3, who may or may not have been Ashley/Amber 2 or 1 but who lived in the separate world of those who secretly know they are exceptionally beautiful, and said with a completely straight face, "You're very fuckable."

"Do you meant that?" she replied, all big eyes and gratefulness. She laughed as she drank her shot of that syrupy stuff frat boys buy girls to prepare them for rape.

Bain was the cocky asshole that made them feel alive, and the cocky asshole that made me sick to my stomach. I was jealous of him and what he's become, of his wife, of his job, of his hair, of the ease with which he can talk to all of the women in this room, but I had to admit, I was impressed. As superficial as I may think he is, Bain believes in what he's doing. He has passion, he has fire. What do I believe in? That I'll wake up tomorrow? That "Buy 2 Classic Novels, Get 1 Free" is an amazing deal? It's a lot easier to believe in nothing than something.

Bain hadn't sold out, he'd bought in. He'd realized his potential, whereas I'd pissed mine away in the pursuit of "something bigger," which is a catchphrase for not really trying anything. Was it a fear of failure or a fear of success that kept me from accomplishing anything tangible? Does it matter? He's got the Armani suit and the hair; I've got worn out Levi's and a jacket that reeks of failure. Though I may not respect what he does for a living, he'd grown into an actual three-dimensional human being and I could only try my best to be one. I thought I was a better person because I had a more pure vision or something but it's obvious that he's the one seeing clearly.

Maybe it was the liquid confidence talking, but it suddenly struck me that having sex with the girl who'd been staring at me earlier was just the thing I needed, that a few hours or minutes or seconds of pleasure with her would save me. "I need to take a leak," I said as I got up from the table, stumbling slightly and causing one of the Amber/Ashley's face to freeze in panic.

I went looking for the staring girl, but she was gone. I sighed and stumbled to the bathroom.

—

Now listening to: "Color Me Impressed" - The Replacements

Subject: Condomania
From: Mike Norton
To: XXXXXX XXXX

I stood in line with other bladder-challenged bargoers, reading cleverly ironic signs in German and possibly Slovakia that were produced in China for an American company to sell to bars and fraternities. I heard a small voice call out my name. "Mike."

I turned, surprised anyone at this bar would know of my existence. A familiar face stared at me. At the time, I couldn't remember the name that was attached to said face. I stumbled over my words. "Hey there... you... it's... good... to see you."

"It's Erica, asshole."

"I know you name... uh, hi."

Erica is a 19-year old from Glens Falls that I'd gone on two dates with a year or so ago. She was nursing some sort of clear mixed drink on ice, seductively slurping it from a red straw.

"I'm surprised to see you at a place like this," she said.

I didn't really want to talk to her, but I wanted to be polite. "I'm surprised to see me here too," I said. "So..." I rambled, my alcohol-filled brain overflowing with stupid. "What brings you to Burlington?"

"I need to take care of something."

"That's cool," I said, desperately try to be exactly that, cool.

Erica looked like she'd put on some weight, and not just in the good places. I'd say something about it being baby fat, but it'd just make me seem like even more of a pedophile than I am for going on a date with a teenager in the first place. "You're looking... wait, how'd you get in here?"

"Mike, I'm pregnant."

Wait. Full stop. Record scratch.

At least the weight gain has been explained. One issue resolved.

My brain became fully engaged. It needed more computational power, so overclocking was enabled. The math started, the counting, the division, the integrals, a square root or two, a possible use of the Pythagorean Theorem just for the hell of it.

We had sex twice, or more accurately multiple times on two separate occasions. It had to have been at least a year ago, right? (Denial, because it's so unthinkable. This can't be happening to me, this can't be happening to me.)

It was still August. We didn't meet last year, that's for sure. It wasn't February or March, because there's no way in hell I'd drive to Glen Falls in the Winter, never mind that we had a sequence of blizzards that left most of the secondary roads covered on snow for both months. So it could've been April, but most of that month featured heavy flooding when the February and March snow melted. So that left May. Yes, it was definitely May.

I started sweating so much it was pooling in my groin. My heart was hitting speed metal tempos and my head felt like someone was crushing it with a vice.

Motherfucking hell, we had six acts of incredibly awkward and unsatisfying unprotected sex sixteen weeks ago. Fucking math. And biology. Miracle of life my ass. (Anger. Lots and lots of anger, resentment, rage, envy, and possibly murderous desires. This isn't not fair, this is not fair.) She told me she was on birth control. Why did I listen to her? Why did I believe her? I had condoms, why can't I get one takeback. (Bargaining. I promise to always use birth control. I'll be celibate. I'll pay penance. I'll go to church. I'll volunteer at soup kitchens. I'll kiss the Papal ring.)

I started to calm down. I was stuck somewhere between being despondent over getting this... this child pregnant (Depression; what's the point of getting upset; I want to curl up in a ball and die) and a warm feeling of elation to find out that I wasn't sterile. (Acceptance. This is going to be okay, we can figure out what to do. Our lives aren't ruined. I get to be a father. Hooray for my perfectly functional sperm and their one successful fallopian run.)

—

Now listening to: "Neil Jung" - Teenage Fanclub

Subject: The Younger Kind
From: Mike Norton
To: XXXXXX XXXX

Is it wrong to believe that age doesn't matter, that, as the
cliché says, it's just a number? There's the idea that the
age-mismatched couples will introduce each other to new
things, that they'll change the way each dresses and end
up going to new clubs and introducing each other to new
music, movies, and other pieces of entertainment or art.
It's solid, right?

Never mind that the older person knows how little
this superficial stuff really matters; it's important to the
younger person, and it's even more important for the
older person to keep them in the dark because being
young is about joy and positivity and exploration while
being old is about being jaded and miserable. It's all a load
of bullshit, right? It's about ego for the older person and
god-knows-what for the younger one. Safety? Comfort?

Parental issues? You tell me. Why were you dating me when you were twenty and I was thirty? (How about we start with I was a young thirty and you were an old twenty and leave it at that?)

So anyway, where do I start with Erica Michelle Burkett, a teenager who lived in another state, for fuck's sake. I made an effort to come out of my shell and ended up a father with a (treated and cured, thankyouverymuch) STD.

She messaged me, I swear. It was to my long-dormant Yahoo personals account. I didn't remember it existed. I replied on a lark. Hah, a nineteen-year-old messaged me. I had no idea why. We struck up a conversation. It flowed well. It was easy. We switched from e-mail to IMs, then to phone calls and texts. She was smart, she was funny. She talked like an adult. She liked things I like. After a few weeks, we decided to meet.

I drove the ninety miles or so from Burlington to Glen Falls, and spent the entire drive saying, "Really?" to myself. It was ridiculous. Too young. I knew that the whole way. But I also knew I'd be a hero to men everywhere for fucking a nineteen-year-old.

You're probably disgusted with me about now, but this is how the male lizard brain works.

Was this too predictable? Was it unromantic? Or was I just happy to go to sleep with a warm body? I decided I was okay with the inevitability of sex. Deciding whether or not to have it, like other things people pretend to regret, wasn't done in the heat of the moment. That happens in books, movies, and TV. In this world, the decision is made when you leave the house, when you talk on the phone, when you close the car door, or when you click on "Reply." I knew we'd spend a couple of hours talking, laughing, eating, feigning awkwardness but waiting for the sex to happen. It would be just like it was with others; there was never any variation in the setup, only in the process and the aftermath. And afterward, there wouldn't be much to say. Neither of us would live up to each other's expectations, whatever they might be.

Only this time it was a bit different, because she was literally a teenager and I literally wasn't one. Unlike the other younger girls I've dated, she actually looked like a teenager, and I looked like a thirty-nine-year-old who shouldn't be dating teenagers. She was, however, cute as a button. We hugged, and she introduced me to her roommate Jenny, who left a few minutes later when her boyfriend arrived. That was the first moment of the night when it really dawned on my that I was actually hanging out with teenagers.

Erica was pleasant but a little distracted. She said she'd spoken with her ex-boyfriend, and it had left her in a bit of a funk.

Her apartment was definitely a college age teen's place. In fact, it wasn't too dissimilar from your own when we started dating. In other words, it was a bit of a disaster. Messy, with all manner of things everywhere. Cheap furniture, clothes, and no embarrassment over its state.

Sitting in the room alone, we smiled. I told her to come over to me. We kissed, she sat on my lap. My hand was up her shirt, unfastening her bra. We ended up in her bedroom, which was even more of a wreck.

"I don't want to do this now," she said.

"Okay."

So instead of having sex, she blew me. This is how teens operate nowadays, I guess.

Her roommate returned a half hour so later, so we decided to go to the movies.

We picked an R-rated movie, and got carded on entrance. Because I was hanging out with teenagers. The kid at the counter checked my ID, looked at me, and said, "Oh, you can all go in." I guess that whole "parent or guardian" kicked in. When the movie ended, we all went to Denny's. Now I was eating food with teenagers. I could be their father.

We returned to her apartment at around midnight. She said I could spend the night, so we got in bed and made out a bit before falling to sleep. We woke up and had sex. Bad sex. Twice. We said our goodbyes.

We continued to chat, she came and visited me in Burlington one night, in her pajamas. Just walked in and we went to bed, had more bad sex, she spent the night, more bad sex. She just wasn't very good at it, which is weird because I'm not any good myself. But she was worse. Because she was a teenager.

She left, and we stopped messaging. A week or so later, I started pissing fire and went for a trip to Planned Parenthood to score some drugs. We'd had unprotected sex that first time, while we were both half asleep, and sure enough, I'd managed to score a gift that kept giving. Chlamydia. It sounds a name people like Bain bestow upon their daughter. "These are our twin honor students Vienna and Chlamydia Bivins."

I had to call Erica and tell her. It went something like this:

"Hi."

"Hi."

"Um, I just wanted to tell you that I have Chlamydia, and you should get checked."

"I've been checked, I don't have it."

"But I haven't been with anyone else for a while."

"Are you saying you got it from me?"

"No, well, probably."

"Are you saying I'm dirty?"

"No, it's not like that..."

"Fuck you!"

And that was that. Not many budding relationships between teenagers and 40-year olds can survive a dose of VD.

—

Now listening to: "My Sharona" - The Knack

Subject: Fallout
From: Mike Norton
To: XXXXXX XXXX

"You're pregnant?" was all I could say.

"Yes, I'm pregnant."

"In a bar?"

"I'm drinking water, asshole."

That was good to hear. She was being responsible and all. But there was still the big question that I had to ask, right?

"Is it mine?" I meekly asked.

"It's not an 'it.'"

"Is the baby mine?"

"What do you think?"

"Oh fuck, oh fuck," I started babbling. All I could think was that this was either a defining moment in my life or a new low, or possibly both running in parallel or ready to collide in some spectacular flaming explosion of death and destruction. My heart was beating, ready to explode. Blood was rushing to my head. I was getting dizzy. I decided to get all righteous and angry. "You said you were on birth control."

"Oh, don't even."

It just kept getting worse for me. "I trusted you."

"Trust has nothing to do with it, asshole," she spat at me. "You should've known better."

"What is that supposed to mean?" Keep digging, my friend. Keep digging.

"You're supposed to be the responsible one! You're old!"

Ouch. Ignoring the fact that she was right, I decided to stick the knife directly into my chest and just go full-on into horribleness. "It's your body!" or some variant, is what I think I said.

Note: I'm not proud of any of this.

Erica threw her drink at me. It drenched my shirt and got all over my face and glasses. Everyone in the club turned around to look at us. I felt extremely self-conscious but also a little bit Hollywood; this kind of thing only happens in movies, right? I licked my lips: water. Thank God. Had it been booze or soda, I would've been sticky and smelly. Things were looking up for me.

"It's not yours, thank God" Erica said as she stood up. "But I'm getting rid of this thing tomorrow, and the other fat fuck who just walked in is going to pay for it."

—

Now listening to: "Walking On Sunshine" - Katrina And The Waves

CHAPTER TEN

There are times when it's clear that a person should accept the situation presented to them, face up to their crimes, and take their punishment like an adult.

This was not one of those times. I fled like I'd been caught smoking behind the gym by the principal. I sped past Bain, who gave me a sort of, "Go, be free young man" wave, though it's also possible it was a "Come rescue me," or "Get out of my life forever," or "Pick up the tab" one. I'm not particularly good with dude body language. Regardless, I chose to take it as an endorsement of my plan to vacate the premises, pronto.

I passed through the cloud of superiority hovering over the bar and finally escaped into the cool and clean night air. I breathed it all in, the throbbing pulse of douchebag reggae no longer kicking me in the nads. I began giggling under my breath, and before long it began to evolve, first into a guffaw and then ending in a full-blown maniacal "Possibly Unhinged Guy Who Stands

Around By Himself Cackling At The Moon" moment. It was as if the world had just played an elaborate hidden camera trick on me and I was finally able to get off screen and enjoy the moment of relief that comes after the moment of abject horror and humiliation.

A woman's voice pulled me out of the moment. "Why'd that girl throw a drink at you?" she asked.

I turned to see who was talking to me and caught a face full of cigarette smoke. I coughed. The staring girl was standing under a tree to my immediate left. I stopped laughing. My laugh-induced euphoria melted away. In the light of the nearby lamppost, I could already tell that she looked like you; they always do. She wore a vintage dress and black chunky shoes. Her lip and right eyebrow was pierced, and the lovely splash of freckles that spanned her cheeks made me think of puberty. I was thinking very bad things that are an affront to feminism and possibly illegal in most states.

"We were just reminiscing," I said. "She's an old friend."

"That wasn't very friendly of her, throwing a drink at you."

"Okay, old former friend."

She pointed in the bar toward Bain. "Your friend there is quite the player."

"He's not really my friend anymore," I said.

"You seem to have a lot of ex-friends at this bar."

"I mean, he's a friend, an acquaintance, yeah..." I mumbled, my voice trailing off when I realized I was completely blitzed.

"You're not doing very well on the friend count tonight."

"We went to college together. We were friends back

then."

"So you're not friends today."

"Not really."

She stretched her arms high up into the night sky and twirled a strand of hair between her finger and thumb in that way that drives obsessives like me mad. "You kinda look like I feel," she said.

"What? I'm sorry?"

"Nervous, uncomfortable."

"That sounds pretty about right."

"Well, me too. I don't know any of these people here tonight."

"You fake it pretty well."

"Thanks, I've had lots of practice," she said before quietly belching. "And plenty of Grey Goose." She giggled.

Maybe it was the alcohol in my bloodstream or the water soaking through my shirt, but there was something about this girl, I couldn't put my finger on it. It just felt right standing there talking to her. I smiled like I was running out of teeth. "I'm Mike."

"Hi Michael. I'm Hil."

"Like Hillary?"

"No, like Hildegard."

"Seriously?"

"No."

I felt myself starting to sweat.

"Isn't it weird how a perfectly fine name like Hildegard sounds like it'd describe a large and homely German woman..." she said.

"...one holding two tankards of ale and wearing lederhosen" I said, completing her anecdote.

"Exactly." She smiled, then leaned in and spoke under

her voice. "Though I have to say, I kinda have a thing for lederhosen."

"I'm wearing some under my pants right now."

"Sexy."

I couldn't figure out why she was talking to me. I was worried that my thin, congealed skin of reasonableness would go glop and expose the boiling sea of crazy that's always threatening to bubble up from below. "Isn't Hildegard actually Dutch?" I asked.

"Do I look like Wikipedia?" she snapped back.

Oh God, I crossed some sort of line. "Sorry, I didn't mean...."

"Dude, chill. You're doing fine. I'm Hillary. Everyone calls me Hil."

I bobbed and weaved, like a boxer feeling out an opponent or possibly someone who'd had too much to drink and was incredibly nervous when talking to age-inappropriate cute girls who were way out of his league. Before I mentioned something about the weather or videogames or something else that would be totally inappropriate and embarrassing, she started speaking again.

"So what are you doing with your life, Michael-of-the-drink-in-your-face?" she asked.

"I'm really trying to do nothing now."

"That's ambitious."

"It takes a certain type to pull it off successfully."

"Hmm," she said, while spinning in place, or at least I think it was her who was spinning. "I had no idea I was surrounded by so many successful people."

"We're a club."

She stopped spinning, or at least I think she stopped spinning. Maybe she was never spinning in the first place.

"Do you have a secret handshake?" she asked.

"We couldn't be bothered to come up with one."

Hil chuckled, but her smile disappeared. "I'm not sure I could be that cool with nothing."

I could tell that the mental calculation of my worth as a person had started in her head, and if the sum were zero, this would immediately end. "I'm just trying to get my bearings, you know?" I said.

"Not really."

"I've got things I'm working on."

"What kinds of things?"

I felt like a fraud, like one of those people who brings up writing or photography in casual conversations as a way to appear deep. I wanted to tell her I that was really a failed writer, a failed photographer, a failed artist, a failed musician, that I could do most things to a level of mediocrity but excelled at nothing.

Instead I told her that I was working on books, songs, blogs, you name it.

"You're just trying to impress me, aren't you?"

"I am," I said. "Is it working?"

"Not in the slightest."

I couldn't tell if she was joking or not.

"Do you go to UVM?" I asked.

"It's complicated."

"You graduated?"

"I'm thinking about going back next semester to pick up a few classes I missed."

"That's cool."

"I guess," she said, looking down. "I'm just putting off the inevitable slide into middle-class death, you know?"

Oh yes, I know. "It's not so bad," I said.

She snorted. "Like you're middle-class."

"You're right. I'm totally starving artist class."

"Living in abject poverty."

"Bingo."

"Now that's sexy."

Did she really believe that, or were we still in the playful banter portion of our interactions? While I was pondering this meaningless detail, I realized that I'd created a lull. The most difficult part of social interaction is managing these lulls. I needed to switch gears, fast.

Hil started talking before I had a chance to assemble a coherent thought. "So are you going to ask me to go somewhere else?" she asked.

"Should I?"

"I would."

"Do you want to go somewhere else?"

She crinkled her nose. "Like where?"

"Somewhere besides here?"

She rolled her eyes. "Hmm, I don't know Michael."

My heart was beating and my stomach was upset, but I was starving. "I could really go for a hot dog right now."

"Are you kidding?" she said, with a look of disgust on her face.

"Yes, kidding!"

I'd blown it. I realized how bad hot dogs sound to girls like this.

"Liar!" she yelled, laughing. "Seriously, you shouldn't eat that shit," she said. "They're full of fillers, at best. Like, would you voluntarily eat anus?"

"I had that for dinner."

"A giant plate of anus?"

"With a side of ranch, for dipping."

She laughed. "Hot dogs aren't good for you, Michael."

"Let me guess, you're a vegetarian."

"I am."

"No exceptions?"

"Well," she paused, with a slightly coy look on her face. She put her hand to her mouth like she was telling me a big secret. "I still eat bacon."

I laughed. "What kind of vegetarian eats bacon?"

"A girl needs a vice."

This was the moment in every conversation when you get to be clever, or at least you say something you think is clever and hope the other person finds you half as clever as you think you are. If it works, you're in; if it fails, it's time to reassess or retreat.

"Okay, Ms. Hil," I said, ready for my big moment. "Can I buy you a bacon latte, an egg roll, some beer, or a plant? Anything?"

She pointed at Bain, who was draping his arm over yet another girl. "What about your friends?"

"They don't seem all that interested in me."

"Fine," she said. "We can go get you a hot dog and me a bagel," she said and pointed her index finger at me in mock schoolmarm pose. "But no more drinks for you."

"No more drinks for me."

"And Michael, I just got out of a relationship, so no falling in love with me, okay?"

It was too late, but I still told that I wouldn't fall in love with her. However, I did ask her if there was still a possibility of sex.

"Michael, what kind of girl do you think I am?" she said with mock indignity. "Sex is always possible."

—

Now listening to: "Party Girl" - Elvis Costello

Subject: Meshing
From: Mike Norton
To: XXXXXX XXXX

It's rare when I immediately mesh and yes, connect, with someone in a random social setting. Hillary and I, our personalities and senses of humor, were perfectly in sync, and I was already falling hard for her. This is the kind of thing that happens when you go without sex for too long. Any scrap of attention—a smile, a simple "thank you," a laugh, a "what the fuck are you looking at, creep"—is enough to create a full-blown disturbance in your anti-love receptors. That person must be your own personal Neo, your very own The One, AKA your Last Chance for Happiness, or the Person With Which You Must Make It Work Or You Will Die Alone. I started to think that yes, Hil could make me happy, while at the same time wondering if I could meet the demands of being happy.

Why can't I stop being like this? Why can't I grow up and become an adult? Why do these questions always rattle around my pea brain? I mean, relationships just continue to baffle me. We were so easy, and now... I don't know anymore. I'm as I've ever been when it comes to the subject of compatibility. It seems like people get together because they're the same or because they're different, and in the end split with each other for the same reasons they got together in the first place. Since we were together, I've tried to be with people whose sensibilities are similar to my own, with predictably disastrous results. Who wants to date their doppelganger? Every quirk and annoyance that you're self-aware enough to know you possess becomes amplified when manifested in your seemingly perfect partner, and the opposite is every bit as hopeless. With nothing in common, you have nothing to talk about, nothing to share. Because I remain in that perpetual post-graduate haze, where opinions on movies, music, books, and concerts matter more than they do to other people my age, it's overly important to me to be able to go the movies with my partner and listen to the same music. Without those things, we're stuck living separate lives and merely sharing a bed, and that better be one goddamn comfortable bed, let me tell you.

I reached that sharing-a-bed point with two people in the ten years since we were us. Ally is beautiful, smart, funny, and loved sex. All we did is fuck. Seriously, she'd booty call me. Me. A few times a week. I know, this boggles the mind. I'm just not that good. She'd show up at my apartment, we'd sit around for a few minutes and make some small talk. Then we'd rip each other's clothes off, have sex a couple of times in the living room or kitchen and go to bed. In the morning, we'd have sex again in the bed, on the floor, or over the sink, and then she'd leave. A few days later, it'd happen again. This went on for nearly a year, and I never got the feeling she cared all that much about me, she just liked having sex. With me. Which again, is patently ridiculous. I guess this is one of those mysteries about human chemistry, why some people's bodies or libidos or minds mesh perfectly at the expense of the others. Ally ended our relationship when I returned from a brief trip to the west coast. This is why I don't take vacations. Fish die, and girlfriends go back to their exes.

A few months later, I met Jeannie. This one hurts more than I'd like to admit. We immediately had a connection and were a couple the day we met, even if we didn't know or admit it. She's funny and quirky and weird and dresses in vintage clothes and Dansko shoes. She's wildly creative, awkward, eccentric, totally insecure, and brilliant. I was crazy for her. Hell, I still am. But she intimidated me, and I always had the lingering feeling that she'd realize that I wasn't clever and smart enough for her.

I also couldn't be there for her when she needed me, and my inability to pull her out of a funk left me feeling like a failure. I don't know how to be the person who says the things you're supposed to say during trying times, and I lack the ability to cheer people up. I couldn't handle her falling apart in front of me, so my inspired solution was to add even more stress to her life by distancing myself from her to the point where I barely existed. When she confronted me over it, I ended things. To this day, it still breaks my heart to even think about it. A few days after we'd resolved to end things, she called me on the phone and just poured out her entire heart to me for over an hour. It was the most beautiful and horrible thing I've ever experienced. She knew things about me that I would never admit to anyone, things I never even admit to myself. I've never felt so exposed before, and I couldn't respond; I didn't have any words left.

I ran into Ally downtown a year after I'd ended things with Jeannie. There was no animosity between the two of us; we ended things on good terms. We talked as if it hadn't been over a year since we'd spoken, that friendly rapport that you can share with people you've slept with. When Ally ended things with me, she told me I wasn't the marrying kind, the man to raise a family with. I never pressed her on what she meant, and had some regret that I never took our relationship seriously, that I just went with the flow and enjoyed the ride, no pun intended. Despite knowing all of this, I had a feeling that our chance meeting wasn't so random at all, that there was some sort of undercurrent to our flirtatious banter. It wasn't just in the conversation, but in the silences. She followed one of those meaningful silences with two words that ended my fantasy: "I'm pregnant."

I started spinning out of control. I threw the usual platitudes at her, told her how amazing it was, how I was so happy for her. And it was true, I am happy for her and the man who probably should've been me. When we went our separate ways, we both said we'd keep in touch but haven't spoken since.

Literally the next day, I got an IM from Jeannie. This was fate, right?

"Hi, this is Jeannie Hampton," she typed. She always used her first and last name. It was one of her most endearing quirks. Seeing Ally made me realize how much I missed Jeannie.

"Hello Jeannie Hampton," I said.

We talked as if I hadn't been over a year since we'd spoken, the friendly rapport that you can share with people whose heart you've broken. I was immediately excited over the possibility that she was re-entering my life. I could see myself having a child, being married. Things were looking up.

"I'm getting married!" she typed.

The cursor blinked.

I unplugged my cable modem and walked away from my computer and directly into a bottle of Goldschläger that had been collecting dust in my apartment for years. Turns out it was for good reason; that shit is nasty.

I ended up in a multi-month funk, the second deepest one I've ever been stuck in. Every day, I repeated this mantra: I don't deserve to be happy. I've never done anything to deserve anything else. I'm selfish, I'm horrible, I hate myself. I deserve nothing, and I'll never have anything.

Jeannie married an incredibly nice guy who is a more successful version of me, and is living a full-blown NPR life of quirk and music and book readings and crafting and fun and clever stories and dinner parties and traveling. Ally has two kids she adores and a husband she tolerates. Both are on my Facebook friends list.

Maybe I should be thankful that there were at least three people who were willing to put up with my shit. Maybe these three examples represent a reasonable number of varied experiences, more than some people, less than others. I don't know. When you view falling in love as the only way to escape the dreariness of your day-to-day life, it's hard to accept that there are no miracles, there's no such thing as fate, and nothing is meant to be. It just is what it is.

—

Now listening to: "All I Want" - LCD Soundsystem

Subject: Meatings
From: Mike Norton
To: XXXXXX XXXX

Hil and I sat on a bench eating our food and making fun
of the bar-hopping hipsters. So many bespectacled, messy-
haired, zero-muscle-tone twenty-somethings! So much
irony! So much smirking! So little caring! So much
dubious facial hair! So much skinny denim! So vintage!
They were sacrificing all of the Pabst money their parents
send them every month for the latest gadgets and fashions
and scenes so they could feel super important and vital,
what with their iPhones and Blackberrys and Macbooks.
Why weren't they blogging? Why weren't they
documenting everything and posting it on YouTube?

"Do you think that shirt comes in men's sizes?" I said,
pointing at one dude.

"I think the key to being cool is a white belt," she said,
pointing at another.

We make fun of hipsters because we too are hipsters, only we're just not trying as hard to not appear to be trying as hard. Or maybe we're trying harder; it's so hard to tell, right? We're just like the average hipster in that we feel like we are somehow magically different from every other hipster, a unique and delicate snowflake in the crushing blizzard that is modern media life. The awareness, and caring about it at all, is a critical part of hipsterdom. In other words, if you spend any time thinking or talking about hipsters it's because you are one.

"You disgust me," one particularly grubby and bearded variety of hippiester said. He was wearing a vintage plaid western shirt, untucked with its snaps unsnapped exposing an ironic AC/DC T-shirt that appears to be sized for a 12-year old. His baggy jeans were covered in real or fashion dirt and stains, and flowed over his new Birkenstocks. I could feel sympathy blisters spawning on my feet; we both know how much of a bitch breaking those things in is, right?

"How can you eat that... that... thing? Do you know anything about commercial meat production...?"

I cut him off because I knew exactly where he was going. Normally, I'd never engage a person who's this far-gone. I'd probably apologize, or apologize and walk away, or just sit there stone-faced and take whatever abuse he intended to throw my way. Tonight, the alcohol was still in charge.

"Yes, meat is murder," I said. "I've read "Fast Food Nation" and "The Jungle" and seen "Food, Inc." I'm eating anus and toenail and intestine and eyelid. It's gross, I get it. Thank you for your concern."

"You're not getting it, man," he said, his voice growing

in stridence and superiority. "Yes, a hot dog is gross, but so are fried muscles, sucking cow's udders, and boiled bird embryos. Plant foods aren't gross and that's what I eat as a vegan."

"Have you ever looked at a cauliflower?" Hil said.

"Oh God yes," I said. "Those things are horrifying."

"Ever heard of a durian?" Hil said. "It's this big scary looking fruit that's supposed to smell like a dead person or feet."

"Yum."

This hippiester seemed a little confused, and possibly stoned. He launched into his pre-planned jeremiad, probably rehearsed for years as ways to get into the panties of the female members of his species.

"A fair look at the evidence shows that humans are optimized for eating plant foods... we're not line animals, we're like... like herbivores. The more meat we eat...."

Hil and I chuckled at the rhyme.

"... The more meat we eat, the sicker we all get. Like heart disease, cancer, diabetes, osteo... oster...." He looked like he was searching his brain for the word. "... that bone problem."

"I was under the impression the average lifespan of humans had gone up over the years," I said.

"Did you know 20 million people will die this year because of the land being used for cattle grazing?"

"And what do we do with all of those cows," Hil said. "I for one am not okay with us starving them to death."

"Unlike people like you, I feel for the other earthlings on this planet. How would you like to be a chicken these days? Humans are the cancer to this planet, if you go on the web to see the Earth from space at night you can see the progression of the cancer on the continents."

I was tempted to throw the obvious, "Why don't you vacate the planet" response, but I was bored. "Oh fuck me, please stop." I said. "What are you going to do, get all vegan on my ass?" I said.

Hil started laughing.

"Assholes," he said, storming off to the rest of his Mexican drug war supporting drug buddies. His type likes to believe he's an artist living outside of the box all of us vulgarians are trapped in, though if the price of admission is that outfit I'm afraid it's a no-go for me. I look terrible in skin-tight American Apparel T-shirts.

"You're a smooth operator," Hil said, interlocking her arm with mine and resting her head on my shoulder. I readied my body for the impact of the inevitable hurt that was about to arrive. I kept holding my breath, to the point where I started to worry that I might be depriving my brain of oxygen. I'm pretty sure it doesn't work that way, but you know I was pretty drunk.

I became acutely aware of the beauty gap between the two of us. She didn't make me feel young and alive; she made me feel bald. I felt undeserving of her. She should be with someone age appropriate, one of those hipsters with white belts and black skinny jeans.

"Let me warn you, my life blows massively right now... it's all just too clichéd and stupid," Hil said. She proceeded to go into excruciating detail about her ex-boyfriend, a 19-year old new media artist from New Hampshire with a "magic dick," according to her, "because sometimes a girl needs some deep-dicking." I'm sitting there the whole time wondering what the fuck she's doing telling me this; is this what kids do nowadays?

"I need hydration," Hil said, and immediately started marching purposefully in a direction. I followed, in line, at full attention.

We ended up at the Green Mountain Co-op Market, which used to be a parking lot last you were in Burlington. When the city was deciding to grant poor people the ability to stay downtown to purchase groceries instead of needing to take public transportation to the suburbs, the wealthy liberals who control the city defied the pick of the poor—the cheap and marginally seedy Price Chopper—and went for the Hail Mary: a giant, organic-friendly, local-farming supporting, co-op. It's a thing of liberal beauty that practically pats itself and its customers on their backs upon entry and says, "Congratulations, you've leveled up in social- and eco-consciousness, and you are a better person for it. Now pay double for all of your social- and eco-conscious groceries, poor person."

Hil made a beeline for the beverage aisle, where rows of colored and flavored sugar water masquerade as health food, thanks to the miracle of marketing buzzwords like "antioxidants" and "acai" and "taurine" and "vitamins." Two girls stood in the aisle shopping and texting with their marvels of modern technology.

"They don't have Blue," one said.

"What about Yellow?" the other asked, never looking up from the warm glow of her iPhone.

"No, they only have it in Green."

"Isn't it a little weird to buy colors, not flavors?" I asked Hil.

"Orange is both," she said. She grabbed something orange.

We walked out the store, and the rhythms of our conversations immediately returned. We talked about some of the classes she took this semester, like "Seminar in North American Environmental History," which told her how evil the white man was when he arrived in these pristine lands, or "Modern Land Use and Environmental Law," which covered property rights, growth management, and wetland protection. "I felt like I was in law school," Hil said. "That, I'm afraid, wasn't sexy at all."

"Isn't that your next step?" I said. "You go to law school and be an environmental lawyer and take on all those evil corporations?"

"Oh God no, at least not for me," she said. "I mean, sure, that's what most of the kids are doing." She stopped to take a drink from her bottle of orange. "The only flaw with this particular life strategy is that they all end up lawyers."

"Ah, and lawyers are evil?"

"Not evil, per se." She paused and tapped her chin with her index finger. "Well, not all start evil, most just end up that way. Whatever, being a lawyer just isn't very sexy."

Hil gave me that anything-goes-feeling, much like you did on our first night together. Though with most girls of this type, "anything" rarely goes.

Still, I wanted to invite her to my place; she probably has other plans, I thought. Everyone under thirty always has plans. "You keep using that word sexy," I said, un-self consciously letting slip a geek reference before going in for the kill. "I do not think it means what you think it means."

"Ah yes, 'Princess Bride,' got the reference. Thanks."

"Does it work for you?"

"Lawyers or 'The Princess Bride?'"

"Take your pick."

"Who doesn't love 'The Princess Bride?'" she asked.

"If you don't love it, you don't have a soul."

"Or are a psychopath," she added.

"Or are Al Qaeda."

"Yes, terrorists hate 'The Princess Bride.'"

"When they took down the terrorists, they were overheard yelling, 'never get involved in a land war in Asia!'"

"Ouch," she said.

"Too soon?"

"We should totally watch 'The Princess Bride,'" she said without even skipping a beat.

"I have it on DVD."

"Let's do it."

"Your place or mine?"

"Yours, but I need to stop at my apartment for a sec and pick up a couple of things," she said. "Do you have a car?"

—

Now listening to: "Hotel Yorba" - The White Stripes

Subject: Running Up That Hil Again
From: Mike Norton
To: XXXXXX XXXX

We'd somehow looped around to the northern most part of Church Street, so we headed south to get my car. I was lost in a bit of a haze at this point. My buzz was fading, worn away by walking and sweating and multiple trips to various restrooms and one alley, but I was still light-headed and the blood sugar rush from the hot dog and bun hadn't been enough the overcome my general tiredness.

Though I was pretty sure I just invited Hil to my apartment to watch "The Princess Bride," I was having some difficulty following the rest of our conversation. It went something like this:

What I said: "So what are you doing with the rest of your summer?"

What I meant: "Will you spend the rest of the summer

with me?"

What she said: "I'm going to Amsterdam."

What I heard: "I'm a drug addict."

What I said: "That sounds like fun."

What I meant: "You're a drug addict?"

What she said: "It's totally overrated."

What I heard: "I'm not really convinced that I want to go, especially since I just met this guy."

What I said: "Why are you going?"

What I meant: "I'm going to talk you out of it by pointing out every single terrible thing about Amsterdam that I can make up, since I've never been there and know very little about it except prostitutes standing in red-hued windows and pot bars."

What she said: "A friend of mine invited me. He's got a place there, and plans on spending his last week stoned."

What I heard: "I have a boyfriend."

What I said: "So that's your boyfriend?"

What I meant: "Fuck. You have a boyfriend."

What she said: "No, just a friend. A bunch of kids I know went on a European hedonism tour, and I didn't have the trust fund to join them."

What I heard: "I don't have a boyfriend."

What I said: "Sorry."

What I meant: "I'm so not sorry."

What she said: "Don't be. If I wanted to save a few bucks I could stay here and get high every day and fuck a different person every night."

What I heard: "I don't have a boyfriend."

What I said: "So when do you leave?"

What I meant: "Please don't leave soon. Please don't leave soon. Please don't leave soon."

What she said: "Thursday."

What I heard: ...

What I said: "That's too bad."

What I meant: "Please don't leave. Please don't leave. Please don't leave."

—

Now listening to: "Candy Floss" - Wilco

Subject: Drug Life
From: Mike Norton
To: XXXXXX XXXX

I still wasn't in any condition to be behind the wheel. "I'll drive," Hil said. "I'm a good driver. " She took my keys and got behind the wheel. After adjusting the seat, she cranked it over. Nothing. She cranked it again. Again, nothing. "Nice ride," she said. It finally turned over on the fourth crank.

She put the car in gear, let out the clutch, and stalled. "I don't drive a stick much," she said.

"I'll teach you."

"Deal."

Hil lived in small house in the North End of Burlington with three roommates and two dogs. She described her roommates as Adam, a part-time student and pot dealer whom she grudgingly admitted to occasionally sleeping with in exchange for weed. There was Karen, who was a vegan with a minor hygiene problem and a propensity for creating, in Hil's words, "The most vile cooking smells imaginable," but who was actually a decent cook of anything made with lentils or tofu. Todd was a Burner who spent most of his winters working multiple jobs in order to take summers off so he could follow around the jam band of the moment, from Phish to moe. to Pearl Jam to another new band which had some combination of food and old-time-sounding music in its name like "Hot Buttered Rum Tin Whistle Hootenanny." There's probably a website that generates jam band names. Whatever.

There was much grinding and stalling and chirping tires for the next mile or so, and I could smell the clutch smoking and burning in agony from the abuse. I'm pretty sure it just earned about 20,000 miles of wear in that short distance.

"Do you want to come in?" Hil asked.

I drummed the armrest so hard my fingers throbbed. I didn't really want to go in because, well, I feared what was inside. But it would be rude not to go in, right?

"Sure," I said.

There were cars parked on the grass, and multiple bikes chained to the porch. A lone weather-beaten bench was uncovered. "I'll warn you in advance, the place is a mess," Hil said as she opened the door.

She wasn't kidding. It looked like a tornado had worked its way across the room, throwing dust on every surface and uprooting every piece of furniture. There was dried mud caked up at the entrance, probably residue from spring, and bite marks on everything from the dogs, or maybe wolves.

"Hey Adam," Hil said. He was sitting in the living room in shorts and a T-shirt smoking a bong and watching reruns of "Alice" on TV Land. The other roommates were nowhere to be found. "This is Mike."

"Hey," Adam said without looking up.

"Wait here a sec, I have to grab something," she said.

I sat down on the least scary portion of the couch I could find.

"You got any cigarettes, man?" Adam asked, finally looking up from his bong.

He's stoned. You can see it in his eyes, in his dilated pupils and pink sclera, in his eyelids sitting lazily at half-mast. "No, sorry," I said.

"It's cool," he said. He halfheartedly extended the bong to me. "You want a hit?"

"No thanks, I'm good."

"You sure? This is some quality shit right here."

"I'm already a little fucked up," I told him.

"Right on, man," Adam said as he went back to staring intently at his bong and managing the complex balance between bud, water, and air pressure. Hil was talking to someone. I couldn't make out the conversation, but she sounded agitated.

I spotted a comic book on the floor. "Did you see the last Superman movie?" I asked Adam.

"Yeah."

"What did you think?"

"Totally gay."

"What do you mean?"

"He looked totally gay."

"The guy who played Superman?"

"Yeah."

"He looks like Superman."

"Superman is totally gay."

"Oh," I said. "Why do you have a Superman comic?"

"Dunno."

"Yo, Adam!" I heard from a male voice in another room. "You got any papers?"

"In the drawer next to my bed," Adam yelled back.

"I'll sell you a gram for twenty," he said pulling out a baggy. "Look at this shit, no seeds or nothing."

"I'm good, thanks."

"This is Hil's favorite," he said. "It'll get you in her panties," he said giggling. "It's blueberry bud. This one time, we're here playing Xbox and Halo and shit, and Hil is just fucked up after smoking this ten spliff shotgun that I invented, and she's, like, talking about her eyes being cold and shit... you ever smoked a tulip or windmill?"

"No, can't say I have," I said, even though I had no idea what he was talking about. For all I know, I smoke those every day, and I don't even smoke.

"You game?" he asked.

"Yeah, I play games."

"I think my favorite game ever is Metal Gear Solid 2," he said, dragging out each word. "For PS2."

"Oh yeah?" I said. "Not really a fan."

"No way."

"Way," I cleverly threw back. "So what's the most perfect game?"

"Pac-Man," he said.

"Nope."

"Tell me how it can be improved."

"Ms. Pac-Man improved it."

"How so?"

"It has a story."

"That's stupid."

"I'm kidding," I said. "It has more mazes."

"Okay," he said, rubbing his chin. "I'll buy that."

"I submit that Tetris is the perfect game," I said. "It can't be improved."

Adam paused. "Hmm, I think you're right."

Hil walked into the room. "Is Adam telling you drug stories," she said as she picked up her keys near the door. "That's all he can talk about nowadays, getting high and playing videogames."

"You're one to talk," Adam said.

"That was me three years ago," she said to me. "I'm not like that anymore."

"Yeah right," Adam said.

"Shut up," Hil said

"I think what's really going on here is that you've got some issues about how I spend my free time," Adam said. "That's not my problem. It's yours."

"I don't have a problem with it, I'm just making a point," Hil said while I tried to move closer to the door. "Are you going to be on your deathbed saying, 'Man, I wish I'd smoked more pot and played more rounds of Halo?'"

"That's a pretty dumbass thing to say," Adam said, standing up to accentuate his point, or possibly to walk into the kitchen to get more food. It's hard to tell with stoners. "I'm pretty sure no dying person wishes they'd spent more time watching 'American Idol' or, like, reading philosophy," he looked down on the comic book on the floor, "I think that when I die I'll feel like a complete moron over pretty much everything I've done in my life." He stood up and knocked some crumbs off his shirt. "In fact, I already feel dumber for having this conversation."

"You and me both, brother," Hil said. "Bye Adam."

"Yeah," Adam said.

"Nice meeting you," I said to Adam.

"Yeah," he said again.

Hil closed the door. "Sorry about that," she said. "I really need to move out and get some better roommates."

"It's cool," I said. "That was fun."

Hil sat down and patted the bench. "Sit down, Michael," she said. "Why are you hanging out with me tonight?"

I didn't really know how to answer. I really wanted to throw the question back at her, because that was much more inexplicable.

"I don't know," I said, realizing that it was a terrible thing to say. "I mean, I'm having a great time, don't get me wrong, but...."

"I know," she said. "I feel like I need to stop doing things just because they feel good."

The conversation got even more casually intimate, though I can't remember a lot of the specifics, and each humorous and self-deprecating anecdote opened a window into how we viewed our worlds. Our previously casual exchanges became packed with meaning, and we grew even closer.

"Look, Hil, this hasn't been a good week... month... hell, decade," I said. "This is a pretty big night for me."

"Aw, so vulnerable," she said with a mock frown, putting her hand on my face. "I bet that gets you lots of ladies." She kissed me on the lips, just a peck, and smiled. "Let's go to your place."

—

Now listening to: "I've Been Waiting" - Matthew Sweet

Subject: Rated R For Nudity, Language, and Strong Sexuality
From: Mike Norton
To: XXXXXX XXXX

Let me tell you a story.

Hil and I ended up at my apartment, we started watching a movie that we had exactly zero interest in actually watching. We stared into each other's eyes for what seemed like hours before I pulled her face to mine and we kissed. We instinctually found the spots we like to have poked, prodded, and nibbled. She almost died when I start kissing her on the neck, and I was more than happy to accommodate her. She climbed on top of me, her face floating above my own. My heart was beating fast inside, and I suddenly became very conscious of her body, of her breasts underneath her shirt, of how I'd be seeing them soon. I could feel the clasps of her bra through the thin fabric of her dress as I ran my hands along her body. I felt the heat of her thighs. I ran my hands across her face and felt her smooth skin. I pulled her shirt over her head and fumbled while removing her bra. She unbuttoned my pants while staring into my eyes. She tried to pull my shirt over my head but it got stuck on my glasses. We laughed, which helped diffuse whatever fear, nervousness, and awkwardness—real or imagined—there was between us. Our mouths breathlessly enacted the desire we felt throughout our bodies and we tumbled onto the bed, removing the bits of clothing we hadn't already removed on the way. She had no modesty, not worrying about the window being open so the world could see our lovemaking. She drew me to her and parted her legs for me. We were in perfect synch with each other. I ran my hand through her hair, which was wet with perspiration. "I was hoping you'd do that," she said. "Now fuck me." We laughed. When you can laugh in bed, everything else should be easy.

Does this sound familiar? It should.

This was exactly what I needed. Hil was put on this very planet to save me. In the movie of my life, this is the exact moment where my misanthropic self starts down the path to redemption. After our night of passion, we become an item. She starts spending more and more time at my apartment. I give her a key so I can come from work and find her in her quirky outfits or still in her PJs, reading printouts of my stories with hand written notes all over them in colored pens. She writes seemingly random messages and attaches them to the refrigerator with ironic magnets; she hangs every scribble and doodle on our walls as if they were fine art. She teaches me how to live again through her eccentric acts of contrived randomness. Why is she with me? Who cares? It's not about her wants and needs. In fact, she has no internal life whatsoever. She only exists to bring light into my dark and dreary world.

Does this sound familiar? It should.

It's also a load of crap. People like to talk about the personal growth that comes with experience, but I'm not buying it. Everything falls apart as you get older, and no impossibly and improbably quirky woman is going to save me. In the non-movie version of my real life, not the version presented here or the one projected on Facebook, I've blown my third act.

I got home at two and went to bed. Alone. Hil and I sat on a bench in front of her apartment and talked, the easy kind of conversation that would make anyone within earshot believe we'd known each other for our entire lives. We exchanged email addresses, hugged, and went our separate ways. I know she would've slept with me if she'd come over to my apartment, but she's only 24 and I'm done chasing 24-year olds. Just knowing that, for a moment, this young and beautiful person was even remotely interested in spending more than a few hours with me was more than enough to satiate me.

And Bane. Bane. Bane. Bane. This is probably how every Facebook reunion ends, with the fantasy of reconnecting and reminiscing quickly wearing off because of the terrifying realization of how much older and uglier and fatter some of us get in 15 years. There are probably examples of people who naturally reattach, but they are the exception rather than the rule. The reasons you drifted apart for those years, those decades, those lifetimes, they were real. You no longer have anything in common with these people; your lives grew so dissimilar because together you dragged each other to the same meaningless center and separately each of you were able to take off to your fate one above or below. At the end, you wonder what you even hoped to discover, and why you even bothered.

I crawled under the covers, safe in the knowledge that I'd feel better the next day. I stared at the invisible ceiling for hours. I looked at the clock radio, it was barely past three. I flipped the pillow to the cooler side. I listened to cars drive up and down Main Street, to the creaks and scuffles from my hundred-year-old building. The night's events were still buzzing around in my head and my brain was in overdrive, spiraling out of control like a popped balloon. Out of nowhere, my feet turned to ice, my arms and face felt like they'd be lit on fire. A tingling sensation shot up my right arm and my breathing grew more rapid, shorter and more labored. I was dying, I thought. I was finally getting what I'd asked for nearly every night for the last ten years, what I deserved. Only now, at this moment, I wanted to take it all back. I wasn't ready. I still had things I needed to do.

—

Now listening to: "Sunday Night" - Buffalo Tom

CHAPTER ELEVEN

Yesterday's doughnuts are still fresh, today's coffee bitter but warm and fragrant. It's nearly impossible to see the text on my monitor because of the glare from the early morning sun.

On days like this, light will occasionally shine into the bedroom or a breeze will blow the curtains of the window and for a moment I'll feel you in the room, and the memory of what it felt like to wake up wrapped around you consumes me. I try to hold on to it for as long as I can, but it inevitably dissipates and I go on with my day.

There are people who say you should get over things, that you should move on, move up, cut your hair and your losses, get a new piercing or tattoo and take off for the bright lights and big city, but what do they know? No matter what I do, you're still inside me, living in my skin and under my fingernails.

The passing of time feels cruel. Ten years ago we were husband and wife for thirteen hours. When your heart stopped beating that night, mine broke forever.

For the first time in days, I stopped typing. I went to sleep and dreamt that I was walking up a steep hill, and when I reached the summit, I could see for miles in every direction.

—

Now listening to: "Someone Great" - LCD Soundsystem

ABOUT THE AUTHOR

Steve Bauman is a professional typist and videogame designer. In a past life, he wrote lots of articles that were published in magazines for which he also served as editor, which explains how they got published. He lives a tragically brooding existence next door to a casino in the uncoolest part of Seattle, WA. This is his first novel.